REAPER

CROW MC #1

By

Michelle Dups

Happy Reading!
Michelle Dups
xxx
2023

<u>DEDICATIONS</u>

To all those amazing single mums out there!

THANK YOU!

Thank you for taking the time and a chance on me, I hope you enjoy reading my books as much as I enjoy writing them. Books make life a little easier to handle in these strange times.

I write what I like to read. Life is hard enough as it is, so there is little angst in my books. They all have a have happy endings, strong family vibes with strong alpha males and strong females.

I am an English author so my American readers will notice a few different words used. As the series goes commences I will publish a list in the front of the books. Please feel free to message me with words you are not sure about and I will add them to the list.

I hope you enjoy reading about my Crow MC family and the life they are building for themselves.

Contents

List of Characters

CROW MC

ORIGINALS - RETIRED

ALAN CROW (SHEP) m. KATE CROW

Children: KANE (REAPER) AVYANNA (AVY)

ROBERT DAVIES (DOG) m. MAGGIE DAVIES

Children: LIAM (DRACO) MILO (ONYX) IRISH TWINS

BELLAMY (BELLA)

THEO WRIGHT (THOR)

Children: MARCUS (ROGUE) BELLONA (NONI)

JACOB OWENS (GUNNY) (First wife deceased) p. BEVERLY

Children: DRAKE (DRAGON) Adopted: ALEC

JONES - DECEASED

ROMAN - DECEASED

CROW MC

1st GENERATION – ORIGINALS

KANE CROW (REAPER) **PRESIDENT** p.ABBY

Children: SAM, BEN, BREN, ELLIE

LIAM DAVIES (DRACO) **VP**

MILO DAVIES (ONYX) **SGT AT ARMS** p. ANDREA (REA) LAWSON

Children: MILA

MARCUS WRIGHT (ROGUE) **ROAD CAPTAIN** p. JULIA WALKER

DRAKE OWENS (DRAGON) TREASURER

7

AVYANNA CROW (AVY)

BELLONA WRIGHT (NONI)

BELLAMY DAVIES (BELLA)

CROW MC

<u>NEW BROTHERS</u>

KEVIN LAWLESS (HAWK) **ENFORCER**

ALAN GOODE (NAVY) **ENFORCER**

SAMUEL ADAMS (BULL) **MEDIC**

<u>PROSPECTS</u>

WILLIAM ADAMS (SKINNY)

TRISTAN JOHNSON (BLAZE)

ANDREW SMITH (BOND)

AMUN JONES (CAIRO)

<u>OTHER CHARACTERS</u>

LEE MASTERS – GYM OWNER

CARLY MASTERS – GRANDDAUGHTER

OLD MAN JENSEN – OWNER OF THE FARM NEXT DOOR TO CROW MANOR

MOLLY JENSEN – GRANDDAUGHTER

WARREN, DEB, DAVID, JULIAN WALKER – JULIA'S BROTHER & FAMILY

BEAU TEMPLE

BOOKER TEMPLE

BRICE TEMPLE

<u>O'SHEA'S</u>

OLD MAN O'SHEA – NONI'S EX-FATHER-IN-LAW

RHETT - NONI'S EX-HUSBAND (IN PRISON)

LIAM

JOHNNY

ADAM

ANDY (YOUNGEST BROTHER SENT TO IRELAND TO FAMILY)

<u>MC OWNED BUSINESSES</u>

TRICKSTER CAFE

CROW INVESTMENTS

STICKY TRICKY BAKERY

CORVUS PUB

CROW GARAGE

CRAWAN GYM

RAVEN ROOST CAMPSITE – coming soon

List of English Words

Twatwaffle – an idiot – general insult

Yum Yums - It's basically a deep-fried croissant, drenched in icing. They are so delicious.

Backpack – not the school kind. This is a woman that is not an Old Lady, Wife or female relative that rides on the back of a bike with a member.

Trackies/Trackie bottoms – Sweatpants

Trainers – sneakers/running shoes

CHAPTER 1

REAPER

Afghanistan – April 2003

Jesus. It's hot as fuck I thought to myself, lying on my bunk and looking up at the desert-coloured tent. The sand drifted through the opening, covering the groundsheet in a thin layer. Both sides of the tent were open, but no breeze was blowing to ease the heat.

I wished I was back home in the small village I grew up in. At this time of the year, it would be lovely and cool and likely raining. I was so dehydrated that my skin would probably suck up the rain. I was getting heartily sick of the heat and sand. It seemed during the last fourteen years, I had been going from one hot fucking sandy hell hole to another.

I had been having thoughts like those more often, and I was thinking it was time to retire. I had never expected to stay in so long, but after 9/11, most of us had re-enlisted.

The foot that I had resting against my knee was hit hard enough to knock my foot off it, and for it to hit the bed. I opened my eyes to slits knowing it could only be one of my idiot friends that were brave enough to do this.

I was right when I saw one of my best friends from childhood give me a shit-eating grin. Liam Davies, also known as Draco.

"You snoozing on the job, Reaper?" he said.

Draco and his younger brother Milo, or Onyx as we had always called him, because the dude had eyes that were as black as his soul. Marcus Wright, known as Rogue and Drake Owens, he got the name Dragon early in his life because of his temper.

Despite us all being in different arms of the military, somehow, this last week, we had all ended up on the same base in this godforsaken hellhole.

We had all grown up in a tiny village in the New Forest called Feannag, which meant crow in Gaelic, which was fitting as most of the village was owned by my family and our surname was Crow.

The story went that my grandfather, after the First World War, had been in London playing in a high-stakes poker game and had won the manor house and all the surrounding lands from a lord who could not pay his debts. My grandfather Kane Crow who they named me after, and some men from his unit made the crumbling manor house their home. Over the years, they fixed it up, and as some married and had families, they renovated different wings to accommodate their growing families. The single men had refurbished a few of the cottages behind the manor. It was still the same to this day, with upgrades done as time passed.

My grandfather bought up businesses in the local village as they became available, and the family still ran them.

They included the Corvus Pub, Sticky Tricky Bakery, Crow Garage and The Trickster Café and Eatery. Out of the original six army brothers that stayed with my grandfather, they each had a son that grew up with my father much the same as I had with my friends. Only four of them remained now, including my father. Unfortunately, we lost two of the men in the Falklands War.

"Rise and shine, you lazy fucker. The CO wants you," Draco smirked at me.

Sitting up, I groaned and rubbed my face feeling my beard rasp against my hands.

"I'm getting too old for this shit," I muttered, standing up and straightening my uniform. Then, grabbing my hat, I shoved it on my head.

"Do you know what it's about?" I asked Draco, who had made himself comfortable on his bunk.

"Nope, but I need to speak to you when you get back," he replied, eyes now closed, hat covering his face. It looked like he was settling in for a long nap.

I walked out into the burning heat, squinting against the sun and cursing myself for leaving my sunglasses by my bunk. I walked over to the tent that the CO had been using as his office.

Standing in the opening, I cleared my throat before saying, "You wanted to see me, Sir."

The CO looked up with troubled eyes. "Come in, Captain. I have news from home."

Usually, my family contacted me directly, but my phone's battery had crapped out on me. I'd planned on replacing it as soon as I returned home. My CO and my dad had been in the military together during the Falklands, and I guessed they had gone directly above me as they couldn't get hold of me. I had a bad feeling in my gut about the news I was about to receive.

"Dog called. He asked me to tell you that Shep is in hospital. He's in a coma. I'm not sure what exactly happened, but they have asked you to come home immediately. I have you booked on the next transport out. It leaves in an hour. Make sure you are on it," he told me.

I nodded, thanked him, turned around and left to return to my bunk. When I walked in, I found all my friends waiting for me.

Rogue had his phone in his hand, and I could see they had more news about what was happening back home.

"What happened?" I asked, grabbing my duffle.

Going to my locker, I start shoving clothes into it.

"According to Bella, there has been an influx of drugs into the area. Harassment and crime are going through the roof. The police, such as they are, can't get a handle on it.

"Your dad was closing up the pub with Avy. He had gone to throw the trash out. She heard noises coming from the back of the pub and got there just in time to see someone dressed in black take a baseball bat to your dad's head. She hit the fire alarm, which scared the guy off. That happened on Saturday night," Rogue said, filling me in.

"Fuck," I bellowed, throwing my head back and sucking in a deep breath.

Shaking my shoulders out, I looked at my best friends. How we managed to all make it through the last fourteen years with only minor injuries was a testament to how good we were at our jobs.

"The CO has me on the next transport out. I'm going to resign once I'm home," I told them.

"That is what I wanted to speak to you about," Draco stated. "I was going to let you know that I'm done. I'm tired of taking too many chances. I've already handed in my resignation. Within the next couple of months, I should be home."

Looking around, I see the others had all made up their minds. They were all nodding.

"Same. We all handed in our resignations nearly a year ago. We'll all be back soon. Don't do anything stupid. Wait for us. We won't be far behind you, then we will clean up the village," Dragon informed me.

Just then, I felt a body gently nudge me, and a set of feminine hands took my duffle from me, emptied it of its contents, and started folding and repacking it. I didn't need to look to see who it was.

I knew it was Cassie Ford.

She was in an American unit. They had helped us out of tight spots a few times. Her unit was the one that got called in when there seemed to be no hope of finding people that have been taken prisoner.

They had saved our collective arses more than once. They seemed to have a sixth sense about them. None of us asked questions about how they did what they did. We were just glad they were on our side.

Cassie was their medic. She was tall for a woman at just over six feet, broad of shoulder and hip, with long dark hair that she usually kept tied in a bun. She had dark brown eyes that saw straight through me. For some reason, this woman always knew when one of us was having a bad day.

"I'm sorry to hear about your dad, Reaper. We'll be giving you a lift as far as Germany," she said quietly.

Something was off about her voice.

A hand reached over and tilted her chin up to us. We could all see the tear tracks and swollen lids.

"Has he been at you again?" Dragon growled.

His face showed how pissed he was.

Moving her face from his hand, she continued folding and packing, finally zipping it up.

"Cassie!" Dragon barked at her.

She sighed, looking at him.

"Leave it, Dray, just ignore them. I don't have to see them very often. Hopefully not for much longer either," she replied.

"What do you mean?" Draco asked.

"Our unit is resigning. My dad wants to retire, and the others won't work under anyone else," Cassie informed us.

I knew she was getting hassled by a rich little arsehole called Ian, which none of us liked. He was ridiculously entitled. He tried it on with Cassie about three years ago and was publicly shot down by her.

Ian hadn't taken it well. He and his cronies were always throwing insults at her about her height, size, weight, and how she only got as far as she did because her daddy was in charge of their team …. all bullshit. Cassie worked damn hard for her team.

We'd all noticed the slurs he threw at her were not done in front of her team. Dragon had gotten in his face a few times and was always disciplined for it.

At first, we thought Cassie and Dragon had something growing, but while he was protective of her and didn't let anyone talk shit about her, she was equally protective of him. On a particularly fucked up joint mission we had been on, she had thrown herself over him during an attack to save his life. They seemed to have an unbreakable bond, but it wasn't sexual.

"I don't know why you don't just punch the fucker," Onyx muttered.

Cassie let out a deep belly laugh. She had a great laugh. It made you happy just listening to it.

"I can't hit him, not because I fear getting disciplined. It's because I don't think I'd be able to stop, and I may kill him," Cassie said matter-of-factly, grabbing my duffle and tossing it at me as if it weighed nothing.

I grunted as I caught the weight of it. Huh, maybe Cassie was right. She would probably kill him.

"Let's go. Jaq has the plane waiting and ready to go," she said, turning on her heel and walking out of the tent. We all followed on behind her.

She was a little way ahead of us when the little fucker started on his cat calling and jeering. I noticed some of his entourage looked uncomfortable, but none of them said anything or stopped him. As Cassie walked ahead of us, we could see how Ian's comments hit their mark, causing her shoulders to droop. I was just about to say something when, from behind me, I heard, "Hey, fuckface."

I saw a blur move, and then Draco rammed into the little prick's body and took him to the floor before laying into him. When Draco was finished, Ian's face was a bloody, groaning mess.

As we walked past, Dragon stopped, held his hand out to Draco and pulled him up off the ground. Then, leaning over, he waited until Ian's attention was on him and then

Dragon raised his eyes to look at the rest of his cronies, that looked like they were ready to shit themselves.

"I am going to say this once and only once. Cassie is off-limits to all of you. If any of us hear you so much as sneezed in her direction, this little beat-down will look like a stroll in the park when we are finished with you." No one said a word. "Do I make myself clear?" he bellowed at them.

We watched as they all nodded frantically, looking like a bunch of bobbleheads. *Dicks.*

Dragon casually walked over to Cassie, threw his arm over her shoulders and walked with Draco on her other side.

"Pick this piece of shit up and take him to the infirmary," I said, turning and walking away towards the transport, waiting to take me home.

I see Cassie's unit waiting for us, grinning. Jaq, their pilot, was jumping up and down.

"Finally, someone put that ass in his place," she whooped, grinning wildly.

"Thanks for the lift," I said.

"No worries, hop aboard," Jaq replied, climbing into the cockpit.

"Let me just clean up Draco's hands," Cassie said, grabbing her first aid kit.

"Babe, they're good," Draco said, holding out his hands for her to see.

"Just let her do her thing, son," General Ford, Cassie's dad, clapped Draco on the shoulder. "It will be quicker. It's her way of saying thanks."

While Cassie sorted Draco out, I said goodbye to all my friends, making notes of messages for their families back home.

Soon we are in the air and on our way to Germany. I would catch another transport home from there.

CHAPTER 2

REAPER

There was no change in the week I was back in the UK. Dad was still in a coma.

While there was no change in Dad, I couldn't say the same about our little village. I had broken up three fights this week in the pub that we owned and was run by my sister Avy. I had run off a couple of punks selling drugs openly in the car park. I felt like I was in the twilight zone.

I felt around my left eye with my fingers. I knew without looking in a mirror that it was swollen. I could already feel a bruise developing. This shiner was from a fight last night in the car park just before closing when a couple of punks decided they would take me on when I threw their drug shit down the toilet. After that, I kicked everyone out and told my sister to close the pub early.

I laid my head back tiredly against the uncomfortable hospital chair in my dad's room. Stretching my legs and crossing my arms, I tried to get comfortable. They could have done with these chairs as torture devices in the war. That's how uncomfortable they were.

I felt a nudge on my shoulder and cracked my eyelid to see a hand with a travel mug in front of me.

"Here, I thought you might need this after spending the night here," my sister said.

Grabbing the coffee from her, I took a sip and groaned at the taste.

"Thanks, sis, just what the doctor ordered."

She snorted and settled in the chair next to me, leaning her head on my shoulder.

I took the time to look at my younger sister, noting the dark circles under her eyes, showing that she wasn't getting much sleep. We shared the same dark brown hair and blue eyes as our mother, but whereas I got my height and size from our father, who was six foot one in his socks, my sister was petite, like our mother, at only five foot two. Although she could pack a mean punch, considering her size when she had to. Before we had all left home, we made sure the girls knew how to protect themselves and worked with them whenever we were home on leave.

"I'm glad you're home, Kane. It's been scary around here lately," Avy said softly.

"I wish you'd said something earlier. We would have come home a long time ago."

She sighed, lifting her head from my shoulders and looking at our dad. "He wouldn't let us. Said you all had to retire in your own time. They are struggling to keep everything afloat, though."

I nodded. We sat in silence for a while, drinking our coffee and watching the machines that surrounded my dad bleep away. It was hard to see him this way. He had always been a robust man. Seeing him like this, I realised how much he had aged since I last saw him two years ago.

My sister spoke softly from next to me, not taking her head from my shoulder.

"They want you to resurrect the MC. They were discussing it when this all happened. Uncle Gunny was going to contact you all against Dad's wishes. We all knew we needed you boys to come back home. Mum and Dad have been arguing about it constantly. Dad wasn't supposed to be with me that night, but our regular bartender had left a message to say he was resigning, as he didn't feel safe working for us anymore, so Dad stepped in."

I didn't know how I felt about my dad not wanting to call us back home. I wished he had. We would have been home months ago before all this escalated. I straightened up in my chair and turned to my sister.

"What do you think of us restarting the MC?" I asked.

A look of surprise crossed her face at my question, and she frowned at me. "What do you mean? The MC has nothing to do with the women in our family."

I snorted at that. "Avy, we all know the women of this family are the face of our businesses. You, Noni, Aunt Maggie and even Bella see and hear more about what is going on in this village than anyone else. Mum works for the local estate agent, so I'm sure she knows just as much as you all do. If we do this, you all must be part of the MC.

I don't care what anyone else has to say about it, so I need your input so we can put it together and present it to the others. I know that Draco, Onyx, Rogue, and Dragon won't have an issue with it, but if we do this, we will need to bring in more men, and they may not get it. It's not usual for MCs to have women as part of them except in the capacity of Old Ladies, hangers-on, girlfriends or whores."

Avy wrinkled her nose at the mention of the last one. "I wish they weren't called whores. All they cause is problems, anyway. Remember back in the day, the one that tried it on with dad and got a fist in the face from mum for her troubles?"

I chuckled, remembering it clearly. I don't think the whore knew what hit her when my mum still in her work clothes of a pencil skirt, jacket and pearls in three-inch heels looking like the well-presented lady, let loose and hit the whore who came with a visiting club right in the nose. There was blood everywhere. The whore had grabbed my dad's junk.

My dad had taken my mum's hand, checked it over and laid a gentle kiss on it before carrying on his conversation. Both had ignored the whore as if she wasn't there. From that day on, visiting clubs were told to leave their club women at home unless she was an Old Lady or long-term girlfriend when they came to visit. Surprisingly, this didn't deter the men from visiting, as my family knew how to put on a good party.

"That's why I want your input on this," I tell her.

"Okay, I think we should be involved in the meetings only regarding what is happening with the business, finances and anything we hear around the village. When it comes to cleaning up and getting rid of the trash, we will leave that to you boys. You are all trained, and we would get in the way. Also, if, God forbid, you guys are picked up by the police and locked up while you are cleaning up the village, it leaves us free to run the businesses. Plausible deniability and all that."

I nod in agreement at all her points. Avy was right. The women knew all the businesses inside out, the people in this village, and what to look out for.

"What about when we ride out? You girls all have your licences. Would you want to join us?"

I watched as she thought about that and finally shrugged.

"I'm not so fussed about riding, and I don't think Noni is too bothered, either. So why don't we play it by ear, and if we feel like it, we join you? Otherwise, I'm happy to keep driving my car, or if we want and you guys don't have any cheap shags riding with you, we can always jump on with one of you."

She smirked up at me and jostled me with her shoulder.

I grinned back at her and pushed her face with my hand. "God, Avy, I've missed you and your snarkiness. I don't foresee any cheap shags or quality ones in my future, so I will happily give you a ride if you like."

There was a hoot of laughter from the doorway at my comment. Then, looking over at it, I saw Noni standing in the doorway with a bakery box in her hands. Bellona, known as Noni, was Avy's best friend and sister to Rogue.

She was tall at five foot eight, with curves for days, long auburn hair and green eyes. They had both inherited their colouring and height from their dad. Their mother had been one of those whores we had been discussing earlier. She had decided that when Noni was three, mothering was not for her and had taken off with a travelling musician that had played at the pub one night. We never heard from her again. Mum had taken over raising Noni and moved her into our house's wing.

"You've jinxed yourself now, dude. What's the bet that you fall in the next two months and fall hard?"

I shook my head as I got up to take the box from her and pulled another chair over for her to sit on.

"Not happening, brat. There's too much to do with cleaning up our village."

"Okay, Kane, but don't say I didn't warn you."

I just shook my head at her before nodding at the box. "What did you bring with you?"

"Just your favourites, cinnamon rolls, chocolate croissants and yum yums."

I moaned as I picked up a yum yum, shovelling it into my mouth. My eyes closed in bliss as the taste hit my tongue. I loved these deep-fried, plaited croissants coated in glazed icing. They were out of this world bad for you, and I could already see an additional two miles added to my run this evening.

Opening my eyes, I see Avy and Noni looking at me with amusement.

"Should we leave you two alone?" Noni queried, snorting with laughter.

"Shut up," I said, throwing my balled-up serviette at her. "I have had nothing this good since the last time I was home. They don't feed you the good stuff out in the desert."

They finally stopped giving me shit, and we took up our conversation where we had left off. I wanted Noni's take on it and what issues she had been having at the bakery.

She grabbed a notebook out of her bag, and we got serious about what was needed from the club and how it would look.

"First, we need total rebranding. Any MC owned business needs to have a logo. Then, cuts will need to be made, and positions decided on," Noni said, tapping her pen against her lip.

Avy and I nodded in agreement with all that she had mentioned.

"I want all you girls in cuts showing you are part of the MC. They don't have to say *property of* if you don't want them to, but they have to have the MC logo and your name on the front, and I want Original under the bottom rocker. I'd prefer you to wear them all the time until this is cleared up. These fuckers need to learn you are not to be touched. What is the timeline for getting the cuts ready?"

Avy responds with a grin, "Ten days for the first batch and the second batch will be ready in three weeks. Noni and I ordered the first batch the day you arrived home. We have also taken the liberty of re-doing the club logo. We have changed little, just the colour of the writing, and added *New Forest* to the bottom rocker. Show him, Noni."

Noni opened up her laptop, opened up a tab and swung it around for me to see.

I was impressed. They hadn't changed it much. There were two, one under the label of the business logo. It had a grey background, with the image of a crow sitting on top of a pile of skeletons, with *Crow MC*, the name of our village and *New Forest Chapter*, running through it. The second one was what would go on our cuts. It had the same picture of the crow sitting on top of skeletons with *Crow MC* as a top rocker and *Feannag Chapter, New Forest* as the bottom rocker, under that was *Original*.

"These are fantastic, Noni. Go ahead and have one done for each Original, including Bella. I'll speak to Mum and Aunty Maggie and tell them they need to wear their property cuts. I'm going to check in with the boys this afternoon and see when they will arrive. Hopefully, it won't be too long. I need to speak to Gunny. We need to get the bikes out of storage and serviced."

"Already done," Avy replied.

"Noni and I organised all that the first two days you were sitting with dad. We knew you would want them. Mum, Aunt Maggie, Bella, and Noni also cleaned the cottages and got them ready in case you boys brought any others home with you."

I shook my head at them. "And you wonder why I want you in on meetings. You have cut the list of all that must be done in half."

The two of them just shrugged like it wasn't a big deal and picked up their trash. It was nearing five o'clock. Visiting hours were nearly over. Mum would arrive soon to spend the night with dad.

"We're leaving it up to you to get the meeting room sorted, as it's been used as a storage room for a while now. And we didn't know what to do with some of the stuff in there," Avy said as she finished buttoning her coat.

"Okay, we aren't opening the pub tonight, so we can have a look when we get home. I think I want to move the meeting room out of the house, anyway. How is the barn looking at the end of the property behind the cottage?"

Avy grimaced, "I don't know. I haven't been in there for years. I'm too scared there will be bats in there or something. You know it creeps me out."

Noni and I chuckled at her.

Going over to dad, I kissed his head, "See you tomorrow, Pops."

I waited for the girls to say their goodbyes, and we walked out of the hospital. We met my mother as she walked in, dragging her overnight bag. I didn't think I'd ever seen my mother not put together, so seeing her in a tracksuit and her hair up in a ponytail was a bit of a jolt. I could see all this was taking its toll on her. Her blonde hair was now streaked with grey, and her blue eyes had dark circles under them. I'd offered to spend the night to give her a break, but she wouldn't hear of it. She had replied that in the thirty-five years they had been together, they had never slept apart.

Hugging and kissing her goodnight, we continued out into the drizzling rain. Avy had got a taxi to the hospital, so we all piled into Noni's bakery van. It was a squeeze, with all three of us in the front. Luckily, home wasn't far from the hospital.

CHAPTER 3

REAPER

The three of us finally made it to the turnoff for our home. I drove through the open gates and made a mental note that they needed to be closed and security upgraded.

We drove through the avenue of trees and caught glimpses of the house through the trees to the left of us. We could have gone straight to the front of the house. There was a big circular drive leading up to the front door. However, that was where we sent guests. The family had parking spots around the back of the house.

If we had driven to the front of the house, we would have seen a beautiful Georgian Manor House in a soft brown stone with ivy and jasmine climbing up the walls and around the windows. The windows are tall and surrounded by white window frames. The front door was wide, as was fitting for a manor house. I had been told that the doors, both the external and internal doors, had all been wide so that the skirts of ball gowns from bygone eras would fit through them.

Whether it was true or not, I had no idea. I knew the front door had been replaced and was now a beautiful sage green, but dad had kept the original knocker and door handle and had them reinstated in the new door.

Instead of turning right to the front of the house, I carried on straight and took the road to take us to the family parking and the garages. Mum and Maggie had asked for the open-sided roofed garage, so they didn't have to scrape the ice and snow off their cars in the winter.

Each family member had a bay for their car and another that housed their bike. For years, it held just the original four MC bikes. Then, as the family expanded, we added spaces as we each passed our tests, including the girls. I parked Noni's van in our parking bay and saw Gunny pull up behind us with Rogue, Draco, Dragon Onyx, and my bikes strapped to the trailers.

Getting out, the girls greeted Gunny as I walked over to the trailer to help offload our bikes.

I hugged Gunny and got a hard clap on the shoulder in return, "Kane, any change in your dad?"

Gunny was Dragon's father and had been in the service with my dad and was around the same age, at fifty-five. He was six feet tall, muscular and fit, his grey hair brushed back from his face and navy-blue eyes.

I shook my head at my uncle while unbuckling the trailer's loading straps.

"No change, Gunny. But the girls and I have been busy this afternoon," I said, looking at him with my eyebrows raised.

He chuckled, "They spoke to you about resurrecting the MC, then?"

"Yep, it seems the women in this family have more balls than the men."

Gunny laughed so hard I thought he was going to choke.

"Son, women have always had bigger balls than us, they just carry them on their chest, and their balls don't affect their thinking," he said with a grin.

I chuckled and grinned back at him as we started rolling the bikes down the ramp until they were parked next to Noni's purple and Avy's blue Sportster. All the bikes in a row were quite a sight to see.

"Where are your bikes?" I queried.

"We moved them into our parking bays. We figured you might need the space if you agreed to reinstate the MC. Also, we were hoping that you might have some recruits from your time in the military."

"I'm going to speak to the boys tonight. I'll tell them what is going on and what the girls and I decided at the hospital. They had better not give me any shit about bringing the girls into this. And anyone who doesn't like that we will have women at the table needs not apply."

"Son, you know that isn't how it's usually done in MCs."

"Gunny, I don't care how it's done in other MCs. This is how it will be done in mine. Our women run all our businesses except the garage. We need them in the meetings. Not just so they know what is going on but also what to look out for. They will be safer if they know what to expect. I don't understand where this idea of keeping women in the dark comes from. They can make better decisions if they have all the facts.

"And as per the conversation we've just had, the women in our family are not shrinking violets. We have taught them how to fight and look after themselves. They have already decided they would only be involved in the first half of the meeting that deals with the businesses, security and finances. Anything that needs doing to sort out this drug problem we have they don't want to know about so that if we get caught, they are still able to run our businesses.

"We have been away for fourteen years, and now suddenly, because we are back, they have no say in what happens with the business they run and their safety? Not in my MC," I declared, breathing heavily and glaring at my uncle.

A round of applause broke out, making me jerk my head in surprise. I looked up to see Avy, Noni, Bella, Aunt Maggie, Dog, and Thor listening to us.

"Spoken like a true President. I'm so proud of you, Kane," Maggie said, kissing and hugging me. "Gunny, stop hassling the boy. You knew he wouldn't leave the girls out."

I rolled my eyes at being called a boy. Avy was sniggering at my look of annoyance.

I'd been had, but at least my sister, Noni and Bella knew how I felt about them joining the MC.

I brought up checking out the barn behind the cottages to use as a meeting room and clubhouse. There would be single guys, and I wanted somewhere they could kick back and relax but not feel uncomfortable like they may have if we used the big house with all the families and couples living there.

"That's a good idea, Kane. It's a massive space, but it's where we store everything we haven't used over the last ten years. It'll need the wiring redone for starters, but let's go look," Thor added.

We all traipsed through the grass to the barn. From the outside, it looked good, but I wondered what the roof and the inside were like. Pushing the doors open, we walked inside.

Gunny found the light switch and flicked it on. The main part of the barn was massive, but it wasn't in bad shape. I think it had been used to hold hay originally. We used to come and camp out here as kids. It seemed bigger then than it did now.

Walking further in, I looked for damp but couldn't see anything. The lights kept flickering. Pushing open the door to the left of the barn, it looked like this would be a bathroom of some sort. Further back, there was a single and then a double door. Pushing the double doors open, I stepped into a large room with nothing in it. I thought that would serve as a meeting room. The last door was just a small storage room.

I walked back to where everyone was standing in the middle of the main room of the barn.

"I think this can work as Church and Clubhouse," I stated.

I got nods of agreement from everyone.

Noni took out her pen and pad and made notes on what was needed.

"First, we need to get the electricity sorted. I will call Abby and see if she can come out to have a look," Noni said.

"Who is Abby," I asked.

"Abby Wright, her dad, owned *Bright Spark Electricity*. When he died a couple of years ago, she took over the company. She now has three others that work for her. They're good, don't worry."

"I'm not worried. I was just wondering if she would know a good plumber. There is what looks like it is going to be a bathroom. I'm sure we'll want a bathroom here rather than going back to the house."

"Hmm, good point. I can ask her," Noni nodded her head at me. "I will want a bathroom."

Everyone else left except Noni, Avy and me. We go around making notes and taking measurements. I'm not sure if the original church table will fit through the doors of the room I want to use for meetings.

The three of us would meet tomorrow evening again to see what the costs would be and make up a budget. I had quite a bit put away in savings, and I knew Dragon, Onyx, Draco, and Rogue would add money.

We finally called it a night, as Noni had to be up at four to get to the bakery.

She said that Gunny was going with her, so she didn't have to go alone when I questioned her about leaving in the dark.

We each grabbed something to eat before heading to our rooms.

I had to see if I could contact the others, fill them in on what was happening, and get their thoughts on restarting the MC.

CHAPTER 4

ABBY

The beeping of my morning alarm was so annoying when I didn't want to get out of bed. I groaned and slapped at my bedside table until I hit the off button. I had learnt long ago to use old-fashioned alarm clocks, not the alarm on my phone. It became expensive when you had to keep replacing them because you kept knocking them to the floor when you slapped them off the bedside table.

Sighing, I swung my socked feet to the floor and rubbed my hands over my face and then through my dark brown hair scraping it back from my face. Grabbing the hair tie on my wrist, I tied it up in a sloppy bun. Standing up, I pulled my boxer shorts straight and made sure my boobs hadn't escaped my tank top before going to the bathroom I shared with my fourteen-year-old son Sam. I took a quick shower before entering the dark, smelly pit my son called a bedroom. Wrinkling my nose, I crossed to the window and opened the curtains to let the weak morning sun in. Glancing around at the dirty, strewn clothes on the floor, I rolled my eyes and thought to myself, *'For a boy who can hit a cricket ball every time, he sure as shit couldn't hit the laundry basket'.*

Going to bed, I grabbed his big toe and shook it. My son took after me and hated being woken up and usually came awake fighting. Sure enough, his arms came swirling out of the duvet as he punched the air around him, making me snicker. He groaned at me and pulled a pillow over his face.

"Don't go back to sleep, Sam. We have lots to do today. Can you still help me out this afternoon?"

"Okay, mum. And yes, I can still help you out today," he muttered sleepily, and I could see he was being pulled back under.

Grabbing his big toe, I gave it another tug. He threw his pillow down on the bed and glared at me. I grinned at him. My boy was good-looking and, thank fuck looked nothing like his arsehole sperm donor. My boy was all me from the top of his dark hair, dark eyes and slightly olive skin tone courtesy of my Greek mother. The only thing he got from his father was his height. At fourteen, he was already hitting six feet with the shoe size and appetite to match.

"I'm not leaving this room until I know you are definitely awake. I can't be late today. I will pull this duvet off if I must," I told him.

"I'm naked under here," he smirked at me. As if that would stop me.

"Boy, I carried you for nine months, pushed you out and cleaned that arse up all by myself. Seeing you bare-arsed naked is not as much of a threat to me as it is to you and your embarrassment. You know not much embarrasses me," I told him.

Groaning, he sat up. "That will probably be more embarrassing for me than for you. I am awake now, though, so it's safe to leave. Why are we rushing again?"

I grimaced, "The Jones job is finished, and I don't want to go by myself to get payment. You know what a sleaze he is. I'm hoping with you there. He won't try to feel me up this time."

That made my boy straighten up and look at me, "He did what?"

"Don't worry, I accidentally stepped on his toes with my steel toe caps, and he quickly moved his hand. I don't want to put up with his bullshit today and want to get it over and done with quickly. Brody can't come as he has an emergency call and is going to see Becky and the new baby at the hospital. He isn't even meant to be working today."

"Okay, I'm up. Give me twenty minutes to shower, and we can leave."

"Thanks, Sam, I hate putting you in this position, but Brody made me promise not to go by myself."

"It's no problem, mum. We're a team. I was going to help you today, anyway."

Nodding, I left his room and went to the kitchen to get the coffee machine on for Sam and a pot of tea for me. I grabbed my phone to check my calendar and noticed three text messages from my friend Noni. Seeing it was past seven, I decided to phone her instead of replying to her text to save time.

I got my phone hooked up to my Bluetooth earphones, so my hands were free to continue with breakfast, as a call to this particular friend could last anywhere from two seconds to two hours.

She finally answered on the fifth ring, "Hi, babes, thanks for calling me."

Just hearing this woman's voice always made me smile. She was three years younger than me, but she and Avy had been my rocks. When I fell pregnant at sixteen, all my friends had fallen away. They had found me in tears in the school bathroom when I had come in to take the last of my exams.

Friends of the sperm donor's new girlfriend had said some horrible things about me, and I'd not been able to take it anymore.

Noni and Avy had a few choice words to say when the girls tried to follow me into the bathroom. Avy had called her mum, who had come to pick us up but not before laying into the teachers and the head. I had wanted to take my exams somewhere other than my old school, but we were a small village, and there was nowhere else for me to take them. From that day on, we had been firm friends. The two of them and their families had helped with just about everything, babysitting when I needed to study for my exams to getting my electrician's licence.

Kate and Maggie had taken my mum's place and shown me how to change nappies, bathe my baby and feed him. I didn't know what I would have done without them. My mum had done a runner when I was six leaving dad and me alone. And while he was a great dad and grandad, he wasn't always practical.

Their whole family had stepped in and helped when dad got ill and had left me with a mess to sort out with the company and overdue bills to pay. They and Brody supported me in getting the company back up and running and in the black.

"Hey Noni, I thought it was better to call than to reply to your text message. What exactly do you need? The wiring on the house is good. We checked and replaced it all last year."

She laughed, "I know. It's not the house. Can you come over this afternoon to talk about three-ish? Avy, myself and Avy's brother Kane, I'm not sure if you remember him, need to ask you some questions and get you to check some wiring out at the barn, and we also need a reliable plumber and carpenter," Noni said in a rush, finally taking a breath.

I shook my head. This woman could talk for England.

Grabbing my diary from the table, as I preferred old-school rather than my phone, I looked at what was happening to see it was mostly callouts after meeting Jones.

"Yeah, I can stop over around three. I'll have Sam with me, though."

"That's okay. I will make sure I bring a few things from the bakery for my godson."

"If you aren't careful, he will eat you out of all your profits. Although with you feeding him like you do, it's saving on my grocery bill," I tell her smiling.

She laughed, and we chatted for a few more minutes before I heard Sam clumping down the stairs in his work boots. I let her know I had to leave and feed him breakfast. He grabbed the phone from me and spoke to his godmother for a bit before hanging up and taking a couple of mugs from the cupboard. He filled them while I finished making bacon sandwiches. Then, picking up the plates, I joined him at our kitchen table. Like everything else, we can see the wear and tear on it. I didn't think dad had replaced anything in our house since the eighties, and I wasn't one for decorating, not that I had the time even if I wanted to.

I filled Sam in on my conversation with Noni regarding going over there this afternoon.

"Do you want me to drop you back here, or do you want to come with me?" I asked him.

"I'm coming with. Aunt Noni already said she was bringing me snacks from the bakery. And anyway, I want to have a look at the barn with you. I know I'm young, but do you think they would consider me doing the carpentry?" he queried seriously.

God, when did my baby grow up and become a young man? He had been coming to work with my dad and me since he was six and had picked up so much from us. On one job, when he was about ten, a carpenter made a bespoke bookcase, and my son was hooked. As the carpenter, Larry was a local man. I had arranged lessons with him every weekend. The two of them had recently done a show and had made some serious money with some of their designs.

"I don't see why not. The family knows you. We can also have Larry speak to Avy's brother Kane if he's worried, and you can show him some of the photos of the pieces you sold last weekend. You can also take him to your workshop if you need to."

To say I was proud of my son was an understatement. I had none of the usual bad behaviour you would expect from a lad his age to deal with. In fact, some of the time, I worried that he wasn't having enough fun. He was in his workshop if he wasn't at school or playing sports. I had built him a workshop behind our offices. As our house was attached to our business, I was always on hand if he needed me.

"Okay then, grab your tool belt and tools and let's get going. First to Jonesy, then to a few other jobs, some groceries, and then to Crow Manor."

Locking up the house, we jumped into the work van with our *Bright Spark Electricity* logo on the side of the van. It was a light bulb with a lightning bolt shooting through the middle of it. I remember designing it with my dad when I was a kid. I had been so proud, now I looked at it and cringed, but dad would never hear of changing it.

Checking both ways, I pulled out into the morning traffic such as it was. We drove past the bakery and waved at Noni, who was standing at the bakery window serving a line of people getting their morning sustenance on the way to work. I knew their next stop would be the café.

Getting to the one set of traffic lights we had in our small village, I noticed that the lights were on in the café, and Bella was opening up the blinds and turning the sign around to show they were open. From the corner of my eye, I noticed Sam had sat up and watched Bella as she moved around the café. I felt my stomach clench, *'Oh shit, I wasn't ready for this,'* I thought to myself, nearly groaning out loud.

We'd had the sex talk and how protection wasn't just to prevent pregnancy. That talk had just about killed me, but I wasn't going to leave him unaware of all the pitfalls.

I had never kept from him how he came about. He was aware that condoms were not foolproof, and while I loved him with all my heart and wouldn't change him for all the world, I also told him how hard it had been and that I wanted more for him.

I knew it was coming. He was a good-looking boy with a sense of humour and kindness. The girls at school flocked towards him, but he hadn't seemed interested. He obviously had a thing for older women, as Bella was sixteen and leaving school this year.

"What are you grinning at?" he queried, his browns pulled into a frown.

"Nothing, just thinking."

"You can be so weird sometimes, mum," he said, shaking his head slightly.

Flicking my indicator on, I turn the van into a run-down driveway. I noticed the bins were overflowing again for some reason. Mr Jones, or Jonesy, as most of the village knew him, never seemed to remember to leave his bins out for collection.

I groaned when I noticed his car was not there. That meant we had to go to his club in the next town over.

Muttering, I put my van in reverse and left his yard, deciding to get the rest of our chores out of the way before trying to pin down Jonesy.

CHAPTER 5

REAPER

I had gone for a run early before coming back to jump in the shower. Then, before heading to the hospital to check on dad, I would pop into the café for breakfast with Bella and Maggie.

Last night I had managed to get hold of Dragon and was surprised to find out they were on their way home and would be getting in late that night. We had all had enough leave left to muster out right away. Our discharge papers would all be arriving soon.

I was feeling better about having them all home with me. I had wanted to do some recon tonight, but they had asked me to wait until we could all go. It was too dangerous to go without some backup. They had agreed with me on bringing the girls into the MC, and as Dragon had so eloquently put it, *If fuckers who want to join don't like it, they can fuck right off.*

I mentioned that Noni had organised for *Bright Spark Electricity* to come and have a look at the barn and get it up to spec. Noni said she knew of a good carpenter too. She and her son would be arriving about three-ish to have a look.

Draco knew who I was talking about as he had been the last home on leave nearly sixteen months ago.

He agreed that having them do the electrics was the best plan as their company had great reviews and was local. He then told me that her son was only thirteen or fourteen and that Noni and Avy were the boys' godmothers. That surprised me as they were in their twenties, and I wondered how they had made friends with a woman who had a teenage son. I did recall mention of her over the years, now that I thought about it. But I had never met her. Not unusual as I hadn't made it home often in the last few years. I would wait until that afternoon and meet them then. I didn't care who did the work as long as the price was right and the work was well done. I was concerned about all this and how much it would cost. While the businesses were doing well, they weren't as flush as I would like. I understood it was because my family had refused to bow to the bullies who insisted on providing security for a price to stop the businesses from being broken into and vandalised. That would be the first thing that I would put a stop to.

I had warned the guys that they would hit the ground running. Our first meeting was set to happen in two days on Friday to discuss doing recon, so we knew what we were dealing with.

We needed to open the pub again, and with the others arriving, we could set up a roster so that Avy was never alone at the pub in the evening. We'd need to see if we could hire a bartender to run the eleven to six shift and set up more cameras and better alarms. Our security was about fifteen years out of date.

I had sat down to make notes on everything I had discussed last night with the girls and then again with the guys. By the time it was finished, I had covered two sheets of paper with what needed to be done.

Looking at my watch, I saw that the morning was nearly gone, as it was now ten o'clock. Grabbing my helmet and keys, I left the house and walked out to where our bikes were parked. Swinging my leg over, I sat down and instantly felt better. Starting her up, I took off down our road heading towards the next town and the hospital.

The ride wasn't nearly long enough. As soon as the guys were back and all this shit with the drugs was sorted, we would plan to go on a long ride.

I was pulling into the hospital car park. I parked up and went up to visit with dad. Sitting by his bedside, I told him all our plans and what was happening. I could have sworn that I felt him squeeze my hand, but maybe it was just wishful thinking. Before leaving, I leaned over and whispered in his ear, "Hey, old man. The boys are coming in tonight, and we will start cleaning up this village. You need to wake up so that you can watch."

Squeezing his hand, I turned and left his room, passing Gunny as he walked in.

"Any change?" he asked.

Shaking my head, I paused before replying, "I'm not sure. I could have sworn he squeezed my hand just now. But it may just be wishful thinking."

"I'll mention it to the doctor when they do their rounds this afternoon and see what he says. It could just be reflexes but let's hope he's coming around. The swelling has gone down significantly in the last day or so. So hopefully, he is coming through the other side."

I clapped him on the shoulder and took my leave for the café and some food. I'm starving, and chicken pie and chips sounded good right now. Leaving the hospital, it was drizzling slightly, pulling my zip up all the way on my jacket. I put on my helmet, got on my bike and headed out.

Pulling up to the café, I noticed how quiet it was for lunchtime, but then again, I didn't see many people out on the street like there usually were. It was the school holidays, and the village was generally heaving. It seemed like the drug issue was not just hitting our businesses.

Getting off my bike, I walked into the café and saw Bella behind the counter. She greeted me with a wide grin that lit up her face. I couldn't believe she was sixteen already. Bella was about five foot six or seven, with long black hair and bright blue eyes.

Taking note of who was in the café as I walked up to the counter. The only other person was a lanky young lad with dark hair and olive skin, about sixteen or seventeen. He watched as I walked towards the counter, and then I noticed his gaze seemed stuck on Bella.

"Hi, Kane. Are you here for lunch?" Bella asked.

"Hey baby girl, yep, I have a craving for chicken pie and chips."

"I'll let mum know. Do you want anything to drink?"

"Just water, hun. Bring it to the family table, yeah."

"Will do," she nodded before turning and entering the kitchen. I sat at our family table, back to the wall where I could watch the comings and goings.

The lad at the table in front of me had finished his lunch, cleaned up his space and taken his plate to the counter. He had said something to Bella, and she had blushed prettily before nodding and handing him a bottle of water.

Definitely, something to be keeping an eye on, I thought to myself.

I had just finished my lunch when a group of four lads ranging from mid-teens to early twenties entered, laughing, shouting and pushing each other. I straightened, as did the lad at the counter.

Bella was serving a young mother and her children but turned when they walked in. I noticed how she tensed and paled when she saw them. Her eyes flicked to me as she walked towards the safety of the counter.

She didn't make it. One of the lads grabbed hold of her and licked up the side of her face before thrusting his hips against her. The others were jeering and laughing. He then shoved her at a blond-haired lad who didn't look like he wanted to be there, but he grabbed hold of Bella and held her tightly. She kicked down on his foot and hit back with her elbow, cursing at him. It wasn't shifting him.

I got up as soon as they grabbed her, but the lad in front of me got to her first and let a fist hit the lad holding Bella right on the sweet spot and knocked him out. Pushing Bella behind him, he shoved her towards the counter and Maggie, who had come out from the kitchen.

The lad that had handed out the punch had given no warning before he let loose with his fists. The looks of shock on the faces of the others as their mate hit the floor were fantastic to see.

He looked at the remaining three. They all seemed to know each other.

Bella's protector cocked his head slightly, looking at the rest, "I have warned you before about touching Bella. You don't listen. How many times do you have to hit the floor before it gets through your thick heads? You don't touch Bella ever, any of you."

I was looking over at where Maggie was now holding Bella. Maggie was looking at me with raised eyebrows. I got comfortable leaning against a table just out of their view. I wanted to see how this would play out.

If it were just teenage agro, I would leave it, but if it wasn't, I would step in. However, it looked as if the lad had it in hand. I would love to know who taught him to throw a punch.

"Yeah, who's going to stop us. You and what army, bro, huh? You going to fight against us when we have these," he pulled up the front of his shirt, showing off a handgun tucked in his pants.

I shook my head, as did the lad in front of them.

"You're lucky you haven't shot your dick off. Have you got the safety on?" He shook his head in disgust. "You are a bunch of morons."

I couldn't help but smirk behind my hand. I had to hand it to this lad. He had balls. The gun didn't seem to phase him at all. I noticed a small smile on Maggie's face. Bella was wiping her face with a wet cloth, a look of disgust on her face, her eyes never leaving the scene in front of her. Worry was clear on her face.

"We may be morons, but we have money, and there are more of us than you. Who's to say we don't visit your mama when she's alone or catch your little plaything in here when she's alone closing up, huh? You can't be everywhere, dude. There are more of us than you. I bet your mama would like some of this," he said, grabbing hold of his dick and thrusting his hips.

I expected the lad in front of me to go ballistic at the mention of his mother. But, instead, what he did was worse. He laughed, and it was a deep belly laugh.

"Chad, I would like to see you try it with my mother. She would eat you for breakfast and still have enough energy to bury your body. Please try it but let me know first because I want to watch her put your arse in its place." He shook his head, hands on his hips, making himself look bigger.

Good tactic, I thought to myself, having used it a few times myself.

The lad that had been knocked out was waking up, and as he got up off the floor, I saw a flash of a knife as he swung it towards the lad who had knocked him out.

Pushing off the counter, I knocked the dark-haired lad into the counter. Grabbing the hand with the knife, I twisted it until the lad was on his knees on the floor. Disarming him, I handed the knife to the lad by the counter.

"Hold on to that for me," I told him.

"What the fuck?" the one that had licked Bella exclaimed. "Where did he come from?"

The one in dreadlocks that had been mouthing off to the lad I had handed the knife to and seemed to be the leader spoke up.

"Man, you don't want to get involved, yeah. Just piss off back to where you came from, and this won't go any further."

The one on the floor was whimpering. *It hadn't been his day,* I thought to myself with an inward chuckle.

"Really? It's not my problem that you are threatening young girls and women with sexual assault?" I questioned, keeping my tone mild.

They all shook their heads, "Dude, this is ACES territory, and the boss doesn't take kindly to strangers interfering in his business."

I nodded my head slightly as if I was surprised by this news.

"Huh, I thought this was Crow territory."

There was sniggering from all of them.

"Who the fuck are the Crows, man? They're a bunch of old geezers that have had their time. ACES are in charge of this village now.

"Hey, do you want to join us? We could use a man like you that knows some moves. The money is good. Just say Chad sent you."

I let him finish his spiel, helping the lad up from the floor. I dusted him down.

"So, you guys are recruiting? Interesting."

I finished dusting the lad off. All of them were carrying except this one. I wondered if this was some type of initiation.

Holding him by the lapels of his jacket, I pulled him towards me and up on his toes, so my face was right in his. Softly I asked him, letting him see in my face why they called me Reaper. "Tell me, was this your initiation?"

He nodded at me, his eyes wide in terror.

"And what were you going to do to Bella?"

There was a bunch of muttering from the others. Then, raising my eyes from the lad I was holding, I looked at the others.

"I want to know what I would have to do if I decided to join your gang. What my initiation would be."

The lad I was holding was shaking so hard I thought he would come out of his skin.

From behind me, I heard the lad who protected Bella say in disgust, "Christ, Ben, you've peed yourself. What the fuck made you think you could be in a gang?"

"Sam, language," my Aunt Maggie berated him.

Well, at least I now knew his name.

Turning my attention back to the lad in my hold, I shook him slightly, "So, what was your initiation."

"They make us do stuff we don't want to do. I was to rape Bella. I have sisters that I have to keep safe. They know that would be the one thing I would struggle to do. If you pass your initiation doing the one thing you hate doing the most, you are in. They film you, so they have proof."

"And you thought the middle of the day would be a good time?" I asked in disbelief.

"Nobody was supposed to be here with her except her mum. We knew Sam would be out with his mum on a job and the lunch hour was dead. The ACES had made sure of it."

"What did they threaten you with?"

From the gang behind him, I heard one of them caution him, "Ben, you do this, and you are out. You know what they will do, dude."

"Don't listen to him, Ben. Tell me what the threat was."

"They were going to use my sisters as whores. Ellie is only eight, and Bren is twelve. I couldn't let them be hurt," he mumbled.

"No, you couldn't. Where are your folks?" I questioned.

"Drunk or high, mostly. They don't give a shit about the girls or me."

"How old are you, Ben?"

"I'm fourteen, nearly fifteen."

Letting him gently back down until his feet touched the floor. I had felt how thin he was under his clothes.

Meeting the gaze of the leader of this little posse over his head. "This is what is going to happen, lads, so listen well, I'm only going to say this shit once."

"You will wait an hour before checking in with your boss. When you do, tell him this is Crow MC territory. Anybody entering this village starting shit will meet with my brothers and me.

"You tell him Reaper, or if he wants my legal name, then Kane Crow says this ends now before any more people get hurt. This is the only warning he gets. He continues to send little fucks to harass my family, and he will get what's coming to him. My brothers and I have just spent fourteen years in every shithole the military wanted to send us to. Going to war on home turf will be a breeze compared to Afghanistan."

No one said anything.

"Did you get all of that?" I asked, still talking quietly.

They all nodded.

"Right, well fuck off then, but remember one hour before calling, and I will know if you call one-second sooner. I have eyes on you."

They scurried out the door, and I grabbed Ben as he went to leave.

"Not you."

He was still shaking, but as I watched, I saw him pull back his shoulders and straighten up, ready to take whatever I was handing out. He was a good-looking lad, if a bit dirty and smelly, in ill-fitting clothes with hair so blond it was almost white and clear blue eyes.

"First, you will apologise to Bella for what you did. And to Sam for trying to stab him. Then you will go with my uncles Gunny and Dog, pick up your sisters, and we'll take them back to the manor where you will all be safe. But before all that, I want you to hear me and hear me good. This is the only chance you get. I find you bringing shit into my family home, then I will see you in the ground. Do you understand me?" I warned him.

"Yes, sir. I just want my sisters safe."

"Okay then," turning around, I looked at my family to ask them to call Gunny and Dog.

"Already on it, Kane," my aunt said, holding up the phone.

Ben walked up to Bella, who was now safe behind the counter. I couldn't help but notice how Sam tensed when he got closer to her.

"Bella, I'm sorry. I wouldn't have gone through with it if it is any consolation. I just needed to keep my sisters safe. They're still babies."

I could see Bella's face soften.

"Apology accepted, Ben. You should have come to us rather than trying to sort this out yourself. That's why Kane, my brothers and cousins are coming home."

Ben snorted, "Bells, no one can get near you between Sam and Alec. They have everyone warned away from you. Everyone knows not to mess with you."

Bella turned to glare at Sam and yelled at him, "What the hell Sam? I'm older than you. Where do you get off warning people away from me? I can look after myself."

I gave him props. He didn't back down from Bella and met her glare with one of his own.

"You're too nice, Bells. If Alec and I weren't watching over you, people would keep taking you for granted and using you. You can't say no to anything, so we do it for you."

"Ugh, you are so frustrating," Bella shouted, throwing her tea towel at him and storming off into the kitchen.

I chuckled, bringing his attention to me.

Holding my hand out to him in greeting, "I'm Reaper. Thanks for stepping in. Quite a right hook you have there."

"Tell me about it," Ben muttered, rubbing his chin.

"I box at the gym down the road with my mate Alec. My mum enrolled me. She thinks it will keep me out of trouble," he grinned at me.

We chatted for a bit so that I could get a feel for the boys. Ben didn't strike me as a bad kid. My gut wasn't going off with any warning signs. The more I spoke to him, the better I felt. I found out the boys are the same age. Sam's age surprised me as I put him at seventeen just because of his size. Alec was Sam's best friend.

Bella came out with a hot drink for Ben and threw him a pair of tracksuit bottoms to change into. She slammed a chocolate cupcake in front of Sam, and he grinned at her making her roll her eyes. I guessed he was forgiven. It was the first time I had ever seen her so feisty. She had changed now that she was grown up. She used to be pretty quiet.

"Here's my number," I said and gave each of the boys my phone number just before Gunny and Dog arrived to pick Ben up.

"Dog, Gunny," I greeted them as they entered the café door. "This is Ben. He's had some trouble," I explained what was going on to them, and they agreed to pick up the girls and clothing for the next week or so. Aunt Maggie had already spoken to her contact at the council and explained the situation. She and Dog were emergency foster carers so that the children would be put under their care. We couldn't keep them forever, but a couple of nights shouldn't be a problem.

"My parents won't even realise were not there. They'll be too high to care," Ben said.

My uncles made a sound of disgust as they took their leave. As they were pulling out of the parking lot, another vehicle pulled up, and a horn hooted from outside the café. In the driver's seat, was a dark-haired woman. My cock perked up and took notice. As Sam grabbed his stuff and shouted out to Bella and Maggie he was leaving, I realised this must be his mother.

Putting a hand on his shoulder as he went to leave, I said quietly, "If you need me for anything, use my number. I don't like the threats those boys made."

He nods, "Will do, Reaper. Mum and I will be over to see you at three, anyway. We're just going to do a quick run to get some money owed by a customer."

He opened the café door and jogged to the van waiting for him, then he got in and started talking.

Her head snapped up at something he said, and my eyes were held by the deepest, darkest, prettiest brown eyes I had ever seen. She wasn't classically beautiful or even pretty. If anything, she had an arresting face with prominent cheekbones and lush-looking lips. There was something about her, though, that hit me just right. I wondered what the rest of her looked like. She blinked, and the spell was broken. She shifted the van into gear and pulled out onto the main road.

I was suddenly looking forward to our meeting this afternoon.

CHAPTER 6

ABBY

Dropping Sam off at the café so he could get himself some lunch, I got the rest of the jobs on my list done before heading to Mr Jones' place.

Pulling the van into a parking lot in front of the café, I went to hoot, but something stopped me. A good-looking, dark-haired man with broad shoulders and an arse that was something to write home about. I wondered who he was. Feelings long-forgotten woke up. I hummed, watching him as he talked to my son and a blond-haired lad at the counter. Dog and Gunny were with them, and I watched as they nodded at what the dark-haired guy was saying.

It seemed that there was a serious discussion going on by the looks of it. Bella came out from the kitchen with a hot drink for the blond lad. She threw what looked like trackie bottoms at him before slamming a cupcake down in front of my son, glaring at him. I raised my eyebrows, wondering what the hell had happened.

Gunny, Dog, and the blond boy left the shop shortly after that. I hit the hooter to get Sam's attention. Turning, he waved his hand before shaking the hand of the hunk of deliciousness in front of him.

He jogged to the van, and once again, I was taken aback by how he had matured in the last few months and how much he was starting to look like a man.

He started talking as soon as he was in the van.

"Mum, that's Avy's brother Kane. He's a badass, and he wants to be called Reaper."

My head snapped up, and I focused back on the café. At the mention of him being Avy's brother, my attention was caught by his burning gaze. I swore my long-dormant ovaries spontaneously exploded at his intense gaze.

I hurriedly put the van back in gear and tuned back into my son's hero worship as he brought me up to speed on what had happened in the café.

It would seem the prodigal sons would all be returning. Both Avy and Noni had mentioned their brothers and cousins over the years. I had seen photos on the manor's walls when I visited, but I had never met them when they came home on leave. The boys had gone to a different school than the girls. When I'd met Avy and Noni, her brothers and cousins were already in the military.

I knew from Avy and Noni that they were going to resurrect the MC, and I wondered how that was all going to work. I guessed I would find out more that afternoon as I was going to be re-doing all the electrics in what was to be their clubhouse.

Pulling into Jones' driveway, I was glad to see his eyesore in the car park. Pulling the handbrake, I turned to my son and grimaced.

"I'm going to try to get him out of the house. He's not dangerous, just lecherous. If he's still not paid after ten minutes, I'll make an excuse and come back with one of the guys. Okay?"

He nodded at me, "Yep, call you after ten minutes."

I sighed, getting out of the car and ringing the doorbell. I had been trying to get the money out of this guy for three months. At this rate, and if things weren't a bit tight, I would be better off just writing the thousand-odd pounds to karma.

The door opened, and Mr Jones was framed in the doorway. He wasn't a bad-looking guy but had almost a sheen of sliminess coating him, much like the oil in his slicked-back blond hair. Mr Jones always wore a suit with a shirt unbuttoned down to his breastbone. He was smallish, about my height but skinny, with acne-scarred skin and pale blue eyes.

"Abby, my love. What brings you to my door?" he stated cheerfully.

"Mr Jones, I've come for the money you owe for the work I did at the club three months ago."

"Of course, why don't you come in, and we can discuss your invoice," he said, opening the door wider and moving aside as if to let me pass through.

"No, that's okay, thanks. I have my son in the car, and we have to be with friends in an hour. So if you could just get my payment, I'll get out of your hair."

His head lifted, and he looked at Sam, who waved at him. He had his phone to his ear and looked like he was having quite a conversation.

About that time, a Land Rover 4x4 pulled up next to the van, and I was interested to see Mr Jones pale slightly as the men got out. They were dressed smartly in black suits with shiny black shoes.

Gone was the cocky man, which made me a little anxious. I turned and started walking back to the van, with Mr Jones following me and going towards the other car.

Mr Jones opened his mouth to say something but was interrupted by Sam, who had got out of the car.

"Mr Jones, I have someone who wants to talk to you. He says he's an old friend. Name's Kane Crow, but you will probably know him as Reaper," he said as he handed his phone to Jones.

The one-sided conversation had my eyebrows raising.

"Hello? Kane, sorry, Reaper. Your woman, you say?" Jones' surprised eyes hit mine.

"No, I didn't realise she was yours. And her boy, he's yours too. Right, right. Yes. No problem. Tomorrow. I understand. Yes, they are just leaving now."

He finished up the call and handed the phone back to Sam. Before turning to me and saying, "You'll have the money in your account by tomorrow morning. You should have said you were Reaper's woman."

I shrugged and opened the door, and got into my van. Then, lowering the window, I leaned out. "It shouldn't have mattered whose woman I am. You should have paid when I asked."

Putting the car in gear, I reversed out of the drive but not before noticing the men from the vehicle surrounding Mr Jones. It made me wonder if I would be seeing my money tomorrow or if we would see on the news that a body had been found floating in the sea.

We left town, and I headed back through the village towards Crow Manor.

CHAPTER 7

REAPER

I made sure Ben was good to go with my uncles, and I was more concerned now than ever. Teenagers from poorer families were recruited. If they didn't do what was asked, their families would be hurt or they disappeared.

Ben had proof of this happening in the low-income area he lived in. I couldn't wait for the others to arrive. Sitting on my arse while more and more people were hurt was driving me fucking nuts. Tonight couldn't come soon enough, but first, I had to get through this meeting this afternoon.

I had just pulled my bike into the garage when my phone rang. Pulling my helmet off, I answered the phone.

"Reaper."

My eyebrows rose in surprise when I heard Sam on the other end.

"Hey, Reaper, you said to call if I thought we needed you."

"That's right. What's going on?"

"Mum and I are here at Mr Jones to pick up the money he owes, but a Land Rover has just pulled up next to us, and I don't like the looks of these guys. Do you know Mr Jones? He goes by Jonesy, and he has a few clubs?"

"Is Jonesy, about five foot seven, dirty blond hair and kinda slimy looking?" I questioned.

"Yeah, that's him. They are walking towards the van now. It doesn't look like he's paid, mum."

I sighed and pinched the bridge of my nose. Bloody Jonesy. It seemed he was still getting into shit, just like he did when we were at school together.

"Put him on the phone, Sam," I said.

I listened as Sam told him I was on the phone.

I hear a surprised "Hello."

"Jonesy, it's Reaper. I hear you are giving my woman the runaround. I don't like it."

He took in a sharp breath.

"Your woman, you say? I didn't realise you've been away for a long time."

"Maybe so, but she is very close to my family, and my sister and Noni are godmothers to Sam. Did you really think this was the first time we had met? Even if she wasn't my woman, she's important to my family, and we look after our own. You know this about the Crows."

"And her son, is he yours?"

"If his mother's mine, then yes, he is mine. Now stop fucking around and pay my woman what you owe her. I want it in her bank account by tomorrow morning or Dragon, and I are coming for you."

"Right, okay, I'll have it sorted by tomorrow."

"Good, and one last thing, if I find out you are involved in any way in the drugs hitting this village and the attack on my father, then you had better make sure you run and run far. Because the boys are home today, and we will be cleaning shit up. Am I making myself clear, Jonesy?"

I heard him clear his throat.

"Crystal clear, Reaper."

The phone line goes silent. I guessed my message was received.

I dropped a text to Sam and asked if all was okay.

"All good, Reaper. We're on our way to you now. Mum's a little pissed. Just a heads up."

I can't help but grin. I was used to feisty females, and it looked like this one was no different from the other females in my family.

I was in for a fun afternoon.

Swinging my leg over my bike, I got off and searched for my sister and Noni. I needed some information on the woman coming over this afternoon to plan my moves.

It had been a long time since I had felt like that about a woman, and I hadn't met her yet.

CHAPTER 8

ABBY

It was just coming up to four in the afternoon. We were running late because of Jonesy, and I was using the drive to Crow Manor to calm myself down. Bloody men. Just one word from Kane Crow, suddenly, it was no problem getting my money.

Muttering under my breath, I saw Sam giving me a look from the corner of my eye.

"What?" I snapped at him.

He grinned, looking way too amused about the whole situation.

"Nothing. It's just I've never seen you like this. You never let anyone get under your skin."

'Observant little shit,' I thought to myself.

"Yeah, well, he had no right to butt into my business," I muttered.

"Mum, I called him. I didn't like the looks of the guys who pulled up in the Land Rover. I wanted to let someone know where we were. There is too much bad shi… I mean, stuff is happening right now."

He quickly changed his sentence when he caught the look on my face.

I sighed before replying, "I get it, hun. I'm just not used to anyone else stepping into our business. We've managed just fine by ourselves over the years."

"I know, mum, but accepting help when needed isn't weak. You taught me that."

"Smart arse, throwing my words back at me," I grumbled with a grin.

I flicked my indicator and turned into the drive that would take us to the manor. As always, I admired the beautiful old house as we drove past the front entrance and around to the back.

Pulling up, I noticed all the bikes were parked in the spare garage. Admiring them, I parked the van and got out of the vehicle. Sam was already out and admiring the bikes.

Hearing my name being called, I turned my admiring gaze from the bikes to see who it was calling me. I saw Kate coming out of the back door.

Moving towards her, she enfolded me in her arms in a hug.

"Kate, how are you doing? Is there any news on Shep?" I asked.

She shook her head and smiled sadly at me. This was the first time she hadn't been well put together in all the time I had known her. The toll this was taking on her was hard to see.

"No change yet, love. We are hopeful, though. He squeezed Kane's hand the other day. We pray that he wakes up soon, and that there is no permanent damage," she replied.

Wrapping my arm around her shoulders, we turned and watched Sam as he walked around the bikes, admiring them.

Turning her head, she grinned at me, "He's going to catch the bug, and then you will be buying a bike instead of a car," she laughed softly.

I shrugged and replied, "He can have a bike when he can pay for it himself."

Kate snorted at that, "From what I heard, he made pretty good money at the last fair he and Larry did. I don't think that threat is going to work."

"I know. Dammit," I muttered.

She laughed. We watched as Sam jogged over to us and pulled her into a hug. "Hi, Grandma Kate. Do you think Kane will teach me?"

"I heard you had met him at the café. He's quite impressed by you. I'm sure if you ask him, he will. Now I have a favour to ask you, and you can say no if you aren't comfortable doing it."

"You want me to take Ben under my wing and have him hang with Alec and me," he replied before she could ask.

Kate cupped Sam's face in her hands and looked up at him with a warm smile, "You're a good lad, Sam. Yes, I was going to ask that. He hasn't had a fantastic mother to teach him right from wrong. He's not a bad

102

lad. He just needs some direction. That being said, if you are worried about him and anything he's involved in, let us know, and we'll deal with it. But I think he is so grateful that his sisters are safe for now that he won't be doing anything stupid."

Sam nods at her words.

"Now, Noni has brought a bunch of snacks from the bakery, and they are waiting for you in the kitchen. Make sure you speak to Kane about doing any carpentry he needs to do. And if he's not sure, show him the dresser you built me."

I lit up with pride for my lad. Not only was he willing to help someone else, but he was already building a business.

Sam smiled at Kate's words, "I will, Grandma and don't worry about Ben. Alec and I will sort him. I'm going to see what Noni brought. I'm starving."

After another hug, he took off for the kitchen.

I shook my head as he disappeared. I couldn't believe he was hungry again.

Turning back to Kate, "Thanks for saying that, Kate. He was nervous about asking if the MC would let him do the carpentry."

"He's great at what he does, Abby. I wouldn't recommend him if he weren't," Kate answered.

"Now, I had better head to the hospital so I can get back here. My son has decided we need to help a young lad and his sisters, and I want to help Maggie should she need it."

"Is this the Ben you mentioned earlier?" I asked.

She nodded. "Apparently, the drug gang taking over the village is moving onto our children. Children they know are vulnerable. They initiate and film them, so they have them doing the initiation. Ben has two little sisters. The gang threatened to do unspeakable things to the girls if Ben didn't do as they asked. Both Maggie and I are registered as foster carers. We have a meeting tomorrow morning with the council and will see what can be done. The little girls are gorgeous but so quiet, and they cling to Ben. From what he has told me, he is more of a parent than their parents."

She shook her head in disgust, "Anyway, for tonight, they are safe. I had better get going, and if you want anything to eat, you had better hurry."

I laughed and hugged her goodbye. She got her keys out of her bag and got in her car. I waited as she started it up and waved as she pulled out of the driveway before making my way towards the manor's back door.

Cleaning my boots off, I walked into the bright kitchen. There was a massive table and chairs in the centre. The wide windowsill had an abundant amount of herbs. The cupboards were white with grey countertops, and the walls were painted a light sage green. It was a bright, cheerful room dominated by a man standing at the head of the table, holding a little blonde-haired girl in his arms. She didn't look like she was older than about six by the size of her. The table was surrounded by Noni, Avy and children of various ages chowing down on bakery goods from Noni's bakery *Sticky Tricky Bakery*.

'Oh my god, there go my ovaries again,' I thought lustfully as I took in the sight before me.

Noni looked up and saw me standing in the doorway. She shouted, "Girl, get your arse over here and grab something before the gannets demolish it all."

Grinning and shaking my head at my friend, I walked over to the table, getting hugs from both Noni and Avy standing next to her brother.

Lifting my eyes to his clear blue gaze, my breath stuttered in my chest, and I held my hand out to greet him.

"Hi, I'm Abby."

I felt the warmth of his palm, and a shiver ran down my arm as he firmly grabbed my hand, his eyes never leaving my face. I could feel my face flushing under his intense scrutiny.

"Kane," he stated. "It's good to meet you, Abby."

Hearing a throat clear behind me, I broke his stare and turned my attention from him to the little girl in his arms.

"And who is this?" I asked, smiling.

"This is my friend Ellie. Her brother Ben and her sister Bren will visit us for a while. Isn't that right?"

The little girl nodded her head shyly. She was like a tiny doll, with hair so blonde it was almost white and big blue eyes. She was clean, but you could see that the clothes she had on had seen better days.

Smiling at her, I asked, "So Ellie, what food is good? Did you have some already?"

She nodded at me before saying softly, "The cupcakes."

"Well then, cupcake it is," I said, reaching over and grabbing one from the plate in the middle of the table.

Looking around, I saw the other two children, Ben and Bren. Pulling out the chair next to Noni, I poured myself a glass of milk, got comfortable and started chatting with them, trying to ignore the smirking Kane at the end of the table.

I found out that Ellie was eight and Bren was twelve. I was surprised because I took them more for six and eight. They were both so tiny. Their brother Ben was the same age as Sam, and the difference between the two was apparent. Ben was nearly a foot shorter than Sam. He looked severely underweight. I could see how close the three children were. They were quiet and constantly looking to each other for support.

The mother in me wanted to find their parents and punch them. I would speak to Maggie and Kate to see if I could do anything to help the children, so they are not taken advantage of again.

CHAPTER 9

REAPER

Ellie was the shyest of the three children and didn't speak much. It had taken some coaxing from Ben for her to try a cupcake. Bren and Ben had been a little more comfortable with my sister and Noni sitting at the table drinking milk while they ate. They were filling us in on the situation with their parents, and my blood was boiling.

While the children were clean, they were severely underweight and small for their ages and needed new clothes.

Noni and Avy were arranging to take the girls shopping tomorrow, and I could see Ben was looking uncomfortable at the thought of them shopping. I had a feeling he was worried about money.

I interrupted them and their plans as I could see how anxious he was getting.

"Ben, let the girls go shopping with my sister and cousin. You can help me sort out the new clubhouse as payment. Okay?"

He nodded with relief on his face, "We don't like to take without paying back," he said.

Bren nodded earnestly. "If Ben helps you, Ellie and I can help in the house. We're good at cooking and cleaning. We can pay you back for the clothes that way."

My heart was breaking at the looks on their faces. Ellie was nodding as I held her in my arms.

"I can clean good. Sometimes when mummy is sick, I have to help clean the bathroom," she said softly, her big blue eyes on my face.

Jesus, fuck, these kids. They are never returning to the shit hole my uncles picked them up from if I can help it.

I can see Noni and Avy are having the same thoughts. I was going to push to see if mum and Aunt Maggie could swing it with child services so they'd stay with us permanently.

The back door swung open just then, and Sam came rushing in. First, kissing Avy and then Noni on their cheeks. He rubbed his hands together when he spied the laden table before dropping down into a chair next to Bella.

"Thanks, Aunt Noni. I'm starving."

Noni snorted, "Lad, you're always hungry."

He shrugged and shoved a pastry in his mouth, chewed and reached for another, getting a slap from Bella's hand.

"What?" he questioned, looking confused.

Bella glared at him, and her eyes narrowed to slits, "Rude, is what. How about letting our guests try something else before you take something? Bren may want another cupcake."

I choked back a laugh. Sam seemed to be the only one who brought out Bella's fire. This was going to be fun to watch.

Sam sighed dramatically, looking at Bren sitting across the table from him.

"Sorry, Bren, would you like another cupcake?" he asked.

She shook her head slightly, her eyes bouncing between Bella and Sam as if she had never seen anything like the two of them squabbling.

Pushing the plate towards Sam, she said, "It's okay. You can have them. I've had one already."

Giving her a cheeky grin, he smirked at Bella before grabbing a cupcake and shoving it in his mouth. The boy was like a bottomless pit. I remember those days well.

The back door opened again, and the vision from the van earlier came in the back door.

My breath stalled in my chest as I took in Abby's curvy deliciousness. She was gorgeous with wide hips and thick thighs encased in well-worn jeans. Her waist dipped slightly before curving to her breasts, which were hugged snuggly by her t-shirt. They were no more than a handful, her skin was a golden brown, and she had long curly dark hair. I groaned at the tightening in my groin as she bent over to greet Avy and Noni with hugs and cheek kisses.

For me, she ticked every one of my hot spots on what my perfect woman would be. I had never been one for overly thin women, or women caked in makeup. Give me a woman who looked like she could take a pounding without me worrying about breaking her.

Oh yeah, baby, you are mine, I thought as she walked over to me, her hips swaying with each step.

I took the hand she held out to me and was surprised by the slight shiver that ran over us as I gripped her hand. It was only when I heard Avy loudly clear her throat that I realised we had been staring at each other. Her cheeks pinkened slightly with colour as she let go and turned her attention to Ellie, who was still in my arms.

I heard a little snort from Noni, and my eyes narrowed on her and Avy's grinning faces.

Shaking my head, I put Ellie down on a chair next to her sister and joined in the conversation around the table.

CHAPTER 10

ABBY

I'm not sure what just happened, but I feel like a semi has hit me. I can't seem to stop my eyes from eating him up. Never in all my adult years has a man affected me like this. If I don't get away from this table, I'm scared I may climb over it and attack the man, children present or not.

After finishing my cupcake, I brushed the crumbs off the table onto my plate. When I took my plate to the dishwasher, Bren was already loading it. I handed her my plate before running my hand over her head, thanking her with a smile.

Turning back to the table, I asked, "Right, where is this barn we need to look at?"

Everyone jumped up and started towards the back door, putting on shoes and light jackets.

Huh? It looked like it was a family event.

We trekked to the far side of the property, past the cottages, towards a large barn.

Along the way, we picked up Dog and Maggie. They had just pulled up in the garage when we left. Thor had gone to the train station to pick up the rest of the brothers. There was a buzz of excitement in the air as Kane pulled open the large wooden doors.

Switching on the lights, they started to flicker. I ventured forward to find the circuit breaker to have a look at it. Leaving the others in the main hall while I wandered around, looking for the circuit breaker. I knew immediately it would need replacing to get it up to spec. Pulling out a notebook, I made notes on what needed to be done..

Hearing a heavy tread coming up behind me, I turned around to see Kane in the doorway of the small cupboard I was standing in that housed the circuit breaker and the boiler for the heating.

Walking closer to where I was standing, he questioned, "So, what's your verdict?"

I cleared my throat after I took in a breath. A moan escaped my lips as I got a whiff of soap and man. My clit seemed to be throbbing in time with my heart. *Seriously, what the fuck was wrong with me?*

Lifting my eyes to his, I saw they were hooded, and his chest was now just inches from mine.

"You need to rip everything out and start fresh. I can do the electrics, but you will need a heating engineer to do the rads and install a new boiler."

He nodded knowingly as if expecting this, "Yeah, can you work up a price for us and recommend a plumber?"

I nodded and moved a little closer to him, licking my lower lip slightly, and my throat suddenly dry. I replied hoarsely, "I can do that."

His hand cupped my cheek, and his thumb rubbed lightly over my lower lip, pulling it gently.

"I'm kissing you now, Abby," he whispered in warning, lowering his lips.

I raised to my tiptoes and sealed my lips to his. His groan rumbled up from his chest, and I felt the hardness of his cock against my belly as he pulled me closer to him. His hands left my waist and lowered to my arse. His hand kneaded the softness, making me shudder slightly as my whole body came alive. Kane lifted me, supporting my back against the wall. My legs tightened around his waist, and all I could think was, *where have you been all my life?*

Thrusting his hard cock against my clit I moaned. I rocked my hips along his hard length. His lips left my mouth and trailed small kisses up my neck towards my ear. Then, he nipped my earlobe, making me squeak in surprise. That got a low chuckle from him as he trailed his lips from my ear back to my mouth. Kane sucked my lower lip firmly into his mouth before moving back to my neck and towards my breasts. Just as he was about to get to my now aching breasts, I heard the sound every parent dreaded when they were about to get lucky ......their child's voice.

"Mum, are you guys done checking out the circuit boards and stuff? You've been ages, and the others have arrived."

I had completely forgotten where we were and muttered darkly as I ground my forehead into his shoulder in regret. I was so horny, and my panties were soaking wet. It had been a long, long time since I had a man. Fourteen years to be exact.

"Babe, fourteen years? Really?"

"Crap, did I say that out loud," I muttered in embarrassment as he gently lowered my legs to the floor just as Sam popped his head around the door. His eyes narrowed as he took in how close Kane and I were to one another, but he didn't say anything.

He turned his attention to Kane, "Nana Maggie says to tell you the others have arrived, and you need to get back to the house for supper. Mum, we're staying too. Nana Maggie's orders."

I nodded and replied, "Okay, we'll be out soon."

He tapped on the door, giving us one more long look and left.

"You didn't answer me. Fourteen years?" Kane questioned again in disbelief.

I laughed a little at his disbelief, "Yep, I've been with nobody since Sam's dad when I was fifteen. I had Sam when I was sixteen, and I was too busy raising a baby, then running a company and building it back up for the time to date. Plus, I didn't want to introduce just anyone into our lives. Sam needed stability more than I needed to get laid."

He shook his head and dropped a kiss on my forehead.

"You amaze me. Just so you're aware, I will ask you out, and we'll see where this goes. For me, it's you on the back of my bike, wearing my patch."

Kane grinned at me when I narrowed my eyes at his tone.

"Really? That's where you see us?"

He dared to grin even wider before replying, "Yup, and then maybe in a year or so, my ring on your finger and my baby in your belly."

My mouth dropped open in shock. Seriously this man. "What the hell? We met like two hours ago," I exclaimed.

He nodded, grabbed my hand and pulled me out of the cupboard and into the main hall. "Yup, but when a Crow man knows, he knows. And honey, I knew when I saw you pull up in your van in front of the café that any woman who'd raised a son as awesome as Sam was a woman that I wanted in my life."

He gently pushed me out the doors and locked them before taking my hand and walking us back to the main house.

I just shook my head. I couldn't make my mouth or brain work to get the words out.

The man was insane. Hot, but insane.

CHAPTER 11

REAPER

I was holding back a laugh at the look on her face at my comment. I wasn't joking, though. When we Crow men found our one, we tied that shit down. My dad married my mum ten days after meeting her. Dog and Maggie had met and married within a month.

I could be patient in marrying her, but there was no way I was waiting to slap my patch on her. At the first meeting, I was putting it out there. For now, I would let her get used to us, and I needed to speak to her son to find out how he felt. He didn't need a dad at his age, but I could be a friend.

We had just passed the cottages when we heard the laughter and shouting. I sped up slightly, still holding Abby's hand. My brothers had arrived. Now we could start getting shit sorted in this village.

Mum and Maggie were being passed around for hugs and kisses from the four of them. Draco was the first to notice us coming towards them. His eyebrows hit his hairline as he took in our joined hands. I gave him a shit-eating grin as he walked to meet us. Reaching out, I hugged him. It was good to have them home.

Turning to the beauty next to me, I introduced them.

"Abby, this is one of my best friends, Draco. Draco meet Abby. She's my old lady."

That got me a glare and grumble before she turned her attention to the man in front of us. Her eyes widened, and her mouth dropped open as her head tilted to take him in. I wasn't fazed. Draco always got this look from people who didn't know him.

He was the tallest of us at six foot six, with pitch-black hair, but what got people was his eyes. They were the brightest gold. His parents had been told that a human containing this pigment was extremely rare. Only five per cent of the world had eyes like his.

"Wow," she whispered.

I growled a little and tapped her chin up to close her mouth, her eyes slanted over to me as she shrugged.

"What? He's gorgeous."

Then she sighed as she held out her hand to him in greeting,

"Unfortunately, only this one makes my ovaries clap," she said, smirking up at me.

"Jesus," Draco moaned. "Too much information."

As for me, I couldn't help but take her in my arms and give her a long hard kiss.

We broke apart at the hooting and hollering. Looking down, I saw her eyes still closed with a small smile. Giving her one last squeeze, we turned to meet the others as they made their way over to us.

Mum and Maggie had ushered the kids into the house to finish preparing supper. I introduced Abby to Onyx, Dragon, and Rogue. Noni and Avy were beside themselves with happiness after the show we put on and were both giving me thumbs-up when Abby wasn't looking.

The guys grabbed their luggage from the vehicle, and we headed into the house for supper.

Mum ushered us all into the little-used main dining room, as it was the only room that would seat all of us. I noticed Ben, Bren and Ellie were standing in a corner together. Ben, with his arms around each of his sisters of them, looked a little shell-shocked at the number of people, noise and food that was being put on the table.

Heading over to them with Abby following along with me, I wanted to check on them to see if they were okay. Kneeling in front of Ellie, I look into her wide blue eyes.

"Hey, how are you guys doing? Okay?" I asked.

They all nodded, but they still looked unsure.

It was Bren who finally asked, "Is this real?"

I tilted my head to look at her from my kneeling position on the ground, unsure of what she was asking.

"Is what real honey?"

"All of you like this, no fighting or shouting, no drugs or alcohol, and so much food? I don't think I've ever seen so much food," she whispered.

My heart broke for these three kids, and I wanted to hurt their parents.

Abby pulled her in for a hug before cupping her face and tilting it towards her. Gently she rubbed away at the tears trickling down Bren's face.

"Yes, sweet girl. This is real. You are safe here. All these people are good people."

"We're only safe until you send us back," Ben said quietly.

I snorted and huffed as I got up, picking Ellie up as I stood to my full height.

Wrapping my hand tight around Ben's shoulder, I shook him slightly, and his eyes swung to mine.

"You're not going back if I have any say in the matter," I told him.

"But how?" he asked, looking hopeful.

"Not sure yet, but Mum and Aunt Maggie are working on it."

I took them to the table and had them sit between Abby and me, with Sam on Abby's right. Everyone else took their usual seats we'd all sat in from the day we were allowed at this table for meals. Or as near as possible in Draco's case, as I had pushed him down the table when I had situated Abby and the kids next to me.

Grinning at me, he went around the table and sat in the chair opposite me. We had all just gotten comfortable when Gunny and another lad, I assumed was Alec walked in. This lad was a little taller, broader and more muscular than Sam, with auburn hair, freckles and brown eyes.

I watched as he went around the table, greeting my family with familiarity showing he had been in this house often. He passed by me and headed for Abby dropping a kiss on her head with a murmured, "Mama A," to which he got a sweet smile and kiss on the cheek.

He then went around and made himself comfortable next to Draco, who introduced himself and the others. I sat quietly, waiting. I wasn't sure for what, but I figured something would happen when all three of the children next to me stiffened at his entrance.

After shaking hands and greeting my brothers, he turned to me and nodded before offering his hand over the table.

"Alec," he said as a way of introduction.

Taking his offered hand, I gripped it and answered, "Reaper," and got a nod before he sat down and looked at the three next to me.

"Ben, Bren, Ellie," he said, his eyes softening as they looked at Bren and Ellie.

I sighed, and across from me, Onyx, Draco, Dragon, and Rogue smirked, probably happy that whatever was to come with these kids was my problem, not theirs.

Mum tapped her glass for attention, "Let's bow our heads and give thanks so we can eat. I'm sure you are all starved."

Bowing our heads for grace, the table quietened until there was a resounding

'Amen', and the conversation took up once more as dishes were passed around the table.

Aunt Maggie had made a hearty stew filled with vegetables and potatoes. Noni had brought fresh bread rolls from the bakery to go with it. This was what I had missed the most while away. Family and good food.

I noticed that Ben was dishing up for his sisters and only adding a little to his plate, hardly enough for a growing lad.

During the meal, it had been decided that Ben would join Alec and Sam at the gym tomorrow, and Draco had said he would go with him to have a look. The girls would go with Noni and Maggie for a couple of hours while Abby and I started on what was needed to get the barn up to scratch.

I was right, though. I knew something was coming when Alec opened his mouth about the amount of food on Ben's plate.

"Ben, if you're working out with us tomorrow, you need to eat more."

"I'll be fine," Ben muttered, looking down at his plate, slowly making his way through what little there was.

"Sam and I haven't got time to baby you if you pass out."

The silence around the table was deafening at the stare-off between the two of them. There definitely was an undercurrent between them.

Catching my mum's eye, I wondered if I should intervene, but she shook her head.

There was a scrape of a chair as Bren stood up angrily, both hands on the table as she leaned forward towards Alec. His eyes flared slightly as if surprised.

"He hasn't eaten for four days, you prick. If he eats anymore, he's going to throw up. You don't get to judge, Alec. You left the hellhole we live in."

"You knew where I was, Bren. Either you or Ben should have said something."

"When exactly, Alec? Huh, when? Since you met Sam, you've been back to the estate three times at the most in the last three years. Of course, there's always school. Should one of us have said something at school? When exactly? If you're not in late, you have your face attached to some slag. What do you want? Us to tap you on the shoulder while you get some skank mouth STD and beg for your time? No thanks, not bringing any further attention to us with the fact that we would dare to speak to the oh-so-wonderful Alec," she snorted and her nose wrinkled in disgust as she glared at him.

"It's hard enough putting up with comments we get about our uniforms, having to walk because we can't afford the bus or our shoes falling apart. If it weren't for Ms James, we wouldn't even have school uniforms. She bought our last lot of blazers, putting aside what she could for us in lost property. So, you can take your shitty attitude and shove it where the sun doesn't shine. You have no right to judge us."

Taking a deep breath, she sat down and looked at mum, who had a smile on her face, "I apologise for my bad language and for losing my temper at your table, Mrs Crow."

Smiling, my mum waved her hand, "Don't worry, sweet girl, sometimes losing our tempers is needed. And you can call me Grandma Kate or Grandma. Either one is fine. Now, why don't you come with me, and we'll get Ben a protein shake that will be easier on his stomach rather than him trying to keep down this heavy meal."

My heart swelled with pride at Bren. It seemed she was quiet but ferocious when her family was attacked. These kids, in the course of the day, were slowly winding and pushing their way into my heart.

I caught Draco's eye across the table, and his eyebrows were raised as if to say, *What the fuck is going on with these kids?*

"Meeting after dinner," I told him, getting a nod from them all.

Alec, whose face seemed to get paler and paler as Bren laid into him, had turned his attention back to Ben.

"I'm sorry, Ben, I hadn't realised things had got so bad for you."

Ben lifted his eyes, and you could see the hardness in them as he looked at Alec, then flicked his eyes across to Sam, who seemed to be taking all this in and seemed just as surprised by the fact that Alec, Ben, and the girls had a history.

"Like I said, Alec, it's not your concern. You don't have to worry about me. I'll do what I have to if it means my sisters are safe and happy. Not all of us run away."

With that, Ben cleared up his and the girl's plates, then took Ellie's hand and pulled her from her seat. Turning to me, he said quietly, "Thank you for today, Reaper. I'll be ready to head out at six tomorrow for the gym."

I gave him a nod and watched as he stopped and spoke to Aunt Maggie, he dropped a kiss on her cheek, and Ellie got a hug before they left to go to the kitchen. I knew mum would make sure they were okay and I'd check on them before I headed to bed, as I had asked that they be put in my wing.

Turning my attention to the lad opposite me, whose eyes were downcast, he seemed to have lost all his cocky confidence and looked like just a regular fourteen-year-old kid that had seen too much of life.

"Alec," I barked out to get his attention which snapped to me instantly. His eyes locked on mine.

"You fucked up," I continued. There was a slight groan from the beauty next to me at my language, squeezing her thigh where my palm rested. I got an annoyed sigh, but no comment.

Alec nodded, "I did," he agreed softly.

"You did. But I know, brothers, and it can be sorted. From what I understand from speaking to them and Sam today, you and Ben were once close friends. You can be again. So don't let what happened tonight fester.

"Tomorrow, you will take Ben to the gym and work with him. He's not fit, and he's malnourished, so you're going to have to start slow. Draco will go with and work out a routine. My only stipulation is that you three boys will be doing it together, and you will learn how to have each other's backs.

Because when things go to shit, you need your brothers. You and Sam have had each other. Now show Ben what it's like not to be alone. You got it?" My tone hardened slightly.

"Yes sir, I understand," Alec replied.

"Reaper is fine, Alec, no need for sir," I grinned at him.

"Right! Why don't you and Sam clear up your plates and head out for now? I'm guessing because you are all so familiar here, you know where you are all sleeping?" I cocked an eyebrow in query.

That got a giggle from my sister, who had been quiet throughout all the drama. "Yep, they stay in your wing," she grinned cheekily at me.

Grinning back at her, I replied, "Perfect."

"Thought you'd be happy about that," Noni joined in, looking slightly smug.

There was a small squeak next to me, so I looked at Abby. Her eyes were huge, "You mean I've been sleeping in Kane's bed all these years?" she asked.

"Yep," I replied with a smirk, "And if I have my way, you won't ever leave it."

The rest of the table laughed at the look on her flushed face.

It was Dog who told her with a chuckle, "Abby love, when a Crow man knows, he knows. Reaper took one look at you today and knew."

"So, I've been told," she grumbled to the laughter that boomed around the table.

Mum came back in and took her seat.

"I've settled them in the room across from yours," she told me. "The boy wouldn't let the girls sleep without him in their room, so we made a camp bed on the floor for him. From what I understand, they have had some friends of their parents try to get into the girl's room at the parents' house. So understandably, he wasn't keen to leave them alone in a house with strange men."

This news was not taken well, and a few chosen curse words were muttered around the table, most of them from the women.

Mum lifted her hand for silence before continuing, "He knows that this is not something he has to worry about here, but that lad has been protecting his sisters for so long that it's going to take a while for him to switch off and just be a brother and not a protector. Let him be. He'll see and understand in his own time.

"Before the meeting, I'm saying that these children won't be returning to their house. I've been speaking to my contacts at the local council and their schools. They were all aware that something was happening, but everything seemed normal whenever a visit was arranged, speaking to the three we have upstairs. They made it look like all was normal or at least that appear so. They were worried about being separated if they were taken into care. There is a teacher at the senior school that has been keeping an eye on them in case things escalate. The children trust her. I'm saying that decisions will need to be made, so for now, Maggie and Dog will be their emergency foster parents, but as usual, we'll all chip in. They will be safe staying with us. I need you to know that if the parents kick up a fuss, things may change, so you must be aware that a new plan will need to be made."

I nodded, already thinking of ways to get rid of the parents, and I had an inkling that the rest of the occupants in this room would be behind me, taking them out.

What made me smile and know that I had picked the right woman was the exclamation of, "Oh hell no. Those kids are going back there over my dead body. Kane, I don't care if you have to take out the wastes of space they came from. I'll be your alibi, or I will find someone who will. Those kids have been through enough."

God, she's magnificent. Her face was flushed in anger, her fist clenched, her chest heaving as she looked at me.

Grabbing hold of her, I pulled her onto my lap and kissed the fuck out of her until the whoops of delight from my brothers broke us apart.

My mother laughed, "Well, I guess I'm a grandmother four times over, five with Alec. I'll be sure to tell your father tomorrow. That should wake him up lickety-split."

I sure as fuck hoped so, holding Abby tighter on my lap when she tried to get up.

"Stay right where you are, babe," I whispered to her. "You've made me hard as fuck with your speech. Can't let you up just yet," I said, grinding my hardness against her luscious arse.

She gave a little shiver but settled down, and I tuned back into the conversation at the table. The older generation was getting up to leave, but just before they did, mum turned back to the room.

"Oh, I almost forgot. Before we leave you to make a plan to get rid of the scum that is taking over our village. Mr Jensen next door contacted me today. He wants to sell but wants to give us first refusal."

The farm next door had good acreage. At one point had been part of our estate but had been sold off before we had taken over this property. From what I understood, it was still a working farm. I knew it wouldn't be cheap.

"How much?" I asked.

"One-point-four million," Mum answered. I winced and saw the others doing the same, except for Noni and Avy, at the amount mum had just given us. I knew it was unlikely we could swing that even with us all clubbing together.

"Is he willing to negotiate terms?" Rogue asked.

My mother grinned at him, "Yes, he is. Eight hundred thousand for the whole lot with one stipulation. His granddaughter keeps the house and the five acres surrounding it."

"Why's he selling, and why does the granddaughter keep the house?" Draco questioned.

"He has cancer and has been given four months. His granddaughter is his only living relative, and he wants to ensure she is settled and financially stable before he dies. She's lived with him since she was five. He trusts us and knows we will ensure her safety when he is no longer here.

"Now I know you are wondering about money, mortgages and all the other expenses. My advice, listen to your sisters.

They haven't been sitting on their laurels while you boys have been away. I'll leave you now." With those parting words, she turned and walked out of the dining room, leaving us slightly shocked.

"Fuck. What the hell? I feel like I've been hit by a sledgehammer since we landed. It's been one thing after another," muttered Dragon rubbing his hands tiredly over his face.

Lifting Abby off my lap, I stand with her. "Right, it's been a long day. I was going to go over everything this evening, but you guys look beat. Let's put a pin in this and meet tomorrow afternoon here in the dining room at three to go over everything. Avy, if you have a way for us to buy next door, bring it to the table tomorrow. Noni, same for you. See you all tomorrow."

Taking Abby by the hand, I led her out of the dining room to the stairs that led to my wing. Before we climbed them, I asked, "Babe, do you need anything from your van for work tomorrow?"

Other than the outburst earlier, she had been pretty quiet. Looking over at her, I could see she was tired and wondered what time her day had started.

She shook her head and started up the stairs before answering with a yawn, "No, I'm good. I have my phone, and I've already sorted the jobs for this week, so my guys know what they're doing. They can call me if they need to or have any emergencies."

I sighed in relief and pulled her into my room. I went over to my dresser and pulled out a shirt and boxers.

"Here, babe, grab a shower. I'm going to check on the kids, and then I'll be in. Are you okay sharing the bed?"

She gave me a small smile, taking the clothes from my hands. "Yeah, I'm okay with sharing the bed. It won't be the first time I've slept in it."

I groaned a little at the vision of her in my bed and gently steered her to the bathroom with a small tap on her arse. Then, turning, I left and went to the bedroom across the hall from me. Gently turning the handle, I opened the door.

Ben immediately sat up, looking ready to do battle.

"Easy, lad," I said softly. "Just checking on you. Do you need anything?"

He shook his head, and his eyes drifted to his sisters, who were both fast asleep in the two single beds.

"No, we're good, thanks."

I nodded and closed the door again. A light was on in the room next to the girl's room. I quietly approached the door and could hear Alec and Sam talking quietly. I stood in the darkened hallway listening to them and learning a few things I didn't know.

"Did you know living at the estate was so bad for them?" Sam asked.

"No," I heard Alec mutter. "My mum has never said anything, but then she doesn't live next to them anymore. She moved when I moved out. It was mum that spoke to Gunny and had me move into the back room at the garage. She wanted me away from the estate. She checks on me every week. She's not a bad mum when she's sober, but when she pumps that shit into her system, she forgets everything. But she has always done what she can to make sure I was safe. I feel like shit that I didn't check on them. It would have been easy for us to do. We go to the same school."

"Well, you have the chance to make it right now," I heard Sam say.

"I'm heading to bed," I heard Alec mutter with a yawn. "We've got the gym, and I'm helping Gunny with an engine change. So a busy day tomorrow."

"Uh uh. I'm going to speak to Reaper about doing the carpentry for the new clubhouse. I may have to ask Larry to have a word as he won't know what I'm capable of. Although Grandma says I should show him the dresser I built her."

"Yeah, that would be fantastic if you got the job. Your summer would be sorted then. Can I ask you a question? I've always wondered this."

"Sure, ask away?"

"Why do you call Kate, Grandma, when she isn't your grandma?"

"I don't know. I've always called her grandma and Maggie, Nana. They've known me since I was born and helped my mum loads. It just seems natural. Shep is Grandpa, and Dog is Pop. My mum's dad was Pappy. It's just how it's always been. My Pappy was good friends with the Oldies. I've spent most of my holidays either here or at home. I guess it's just how it's always been. I've never thought about it."

"Huh, okay. You were lucky you had them."

"Yeah, I know, but you've had them the last four years too."

Hearing them settling down and getting into bed, I tiptoed back to my room, closed the door a little harder than necessary, and then walked down the passage again with some noise so that they heard me coming.

Getting to their bedroom door, I tapped on it lightly before pushing it open.

The two of them were in bed looking younger than they did earlier in the day.

"Just checking on you both, making sure you are all okay after this evening."

They both nodded at me before Sam replied. "We're good, Reaper." He hesitated slightly, looking a little uncertain, before asking, "Can I meet with you tomorrow to discuss something?"

"Sure," I replied. "What about after you come back from the gym?"

"Um, I may not come back here. Do you mind meeting me at the shop? If you follow the road around the back, there is a workshop, and what I need to discuss with you is there."

"No problem. I think I'll join you at the gym tomorrow, then we can head to your place, and I'll go to the hospital from there. That good?"

He gave me a blinding smile, "Yeah, that would be great. Thanks."

Nodding, I tapped the door frame before leaving them and made my way back to my room, where my woman was waiting for me.

I smiled when I entered and saw her fast asleep, the covers pulled up tight to her chin, her long brown hair lying wild over our pillows.

I grabbed a quick shower before slipping into bed, pulling Abby tight against me. I pressed a kiss to the back of her head, drifting off to sleep with a smile on my face.

This Crow has found his woman, and as with our wild brethren, we mated for life.

CHAPTER 12

ABBY

I woke to weak sunlight filtering through the gap in the curtains. Running my hand over the sheets next to me, I feel they are cold. The only indication Kane had been in bed next to me was the indentation of his head on the pillow.

I'm not sure if I'm disappointed or relieved that he didn't try anything last night. Shaking my head, I think about what I must do today, including taking the girls shopping for clothes this afternoon. All our plans had been moved around, with the meeting being changed to this afternoon instead of last night.

After a long cat-like stretch, I got up, went to the bathroom, did my routine and then made the bed. Heading to the dresser on the far side of the bedroom, I opened the bottom drawer and found a set of clean clothes I had left here a couple of months ago. I was surprised Kane hadn't questioned the woman's clothing when he moved in. Opening the rest of the drawers, I realised they were all empty. I guessed he didn't use this dresser.

Pulling on the clean underwear, jeans and jumper, I put my dirty clothes in the laundry basket in the corner of the room. Then, picking it up, I make my way through each of the bedrooms to pick up any dirty clothes and get them in the machine. Each floor had its own laundry room, so you didn't have to traipse downstairs with your washing.

Opening the room that Ben and the girls had used, I smiled when I saw everything was neatly folded, beds made, and Ben's makeshift bed tidied up and put in a pile on the chair in the corner. Then, checking their washing basket, I noted it was empty of dirty washing.

Heading to the bedroom next door, I saw it starkly contrasted with the one I had just come out of. The beds were left unmade, and clothes were scattered across the floor. Shaking my head at the mess, I picked it all up and added it to my basket before heading to the laundry room.

I was surprised to find Bren and Ellie already in there, snuggled up and reading quietly on the sofa that looked like it had seen better days but that I knew was very comfortable. Each laundry room had one so you could sit and fold if you wanted to while waiting for your next load to finish.

Smiling at them as I walked in, I said, "Good morning, girls. How are you both this morning?"

They smiled shyly at me, and once again, I was struck by the sheer beauty of these two. They replied with a quiet, "Morning."

Seeing the empty washing machine, I loaded it up and started it. Their washing was already in the tumble dryer.

Finishing up, I asked if they had eaten breakfast, and they both shook their heads.

"Not yet. We weren't sure if we would be allowed to go to the kitchen alone or to take food," Bren replied.

I thought, *'These kids were going to kill me. I didn't think it was so much politeness that had stopped them but the fact that their kitchen didn't always have food in it or they were punished for taking without asking.'* I blinked my eyes quickly to stop the tears.

Clearing my throat roughly, I grabbed their hands and pulled them up from the couch and into my arms. Hugging them both tightly, I told them, "You never have to worry about that in this house, girls. If you're hungry and there is food in the kitchen, you help yourselves and eat. Come on, let's fold your washing and go and get some breakfast."

Grabbing their washing out of the dryer, I helped fold the few clothes they'd washed, and we dropped them off in their room on our way downstairs. Once we got to the kitchen, I showed them where they could find everything, and we made toast and scrambled eggs. Finally, they slowly started to open up and feel more comfortable with me.

"So, what do you girls feel like doing today?" I asked.

"I was supposed to go with Noni to the bakery this morning, but she put a note under the door to say that I was to sleep in and we would start tomorrow. I don't know if there is any cleaning or anything we need to do for Ms Maggie to help her?" Bren said.

"Ah, hun, you don't have to worry about cleaning too much. Just keep your bedroom tidy. Maggie and Kate have a cleaner who comes in and does the heavy cleaning a few times a week."

"Wow, they have a cleaner. They must be very rich," Ellie said, her eyes huge.

Bren and I laughed a little at the amazement in Ellie's voice. I guessed having a cleaner may seem a bit odd to these two. I certainly wouldn't like to keep on top of keeping this huge house clean and tidy. Grabbing our plates, I took them over to the sink to rinse. Bren took them from me and loaded the dishwasher. Looking over my shoulder, I saw Ellie wiping down the table and putting everything back where it should be.

Seriously, *'These kids needed to learn to relax a little.'*

"Well, as you two girls are free for the morning, do you want to come to the barn and help me take measurements and make notes on what I will need to get the electrics sorted?"

They both nodded in agreement. We headed to the back door and the shoe and coat rack. Suiting up, I opened the door and saw it was drizzling again.

"Got to love an English spring day," I muttered, pulling my hood up. Then, making sure the girls were covered, we walked over to the barn along the gravel path past the cottage. I saw they were both in sneakers and made a mental note to see about some wellies for them.

I unlocked it with the key Kane gave me last night to get into the barn. Then, pulling out my tape measure and notebook from my wax jacket's deep pockets, we started work.

I loved spending time with the girls. Once they relaxed, I found them to be bright and fun to be around. When Ellie grew bored, I tore a few pages out of my notebook and set her up with a pencil to draw happily.

Bren and I were in the back of the barn looking at what would be the bathrooms when I heard a little grumble from the tummy of the girl standing next to me. I looked up with a grin.

Bren's cheeks were pink, "Sorry," she whispered.

Looking at my phone, I saw it was nearly lunchtime.

I grinned at her and flicked her nose, "No worries, hun, I'm getting hungry too. We've done loads of work this morning, enough for me to list the stuff we need. Let's grab your sister and head back to the main house to see what we can scrounge up for lunch."

Locking up, we headed back to the main house and found the kitchen filled with a bunch of delicious looking men. No Kane, though.

Draco turned from the stove, where he was stirring a pot of what smelled like tomato soup, and Dragon was at another counter buttering toast.

I greeted them all with a smile as we walked through the door in our socks, having left our muddy shoes in the hallway.

"Hey guys, anything we can do to help?"

Draco shook his head, "Nope, this is nearly ready. Wash hands and grab a seat."

The girls and I cleaned up and sat at the table. Bowls were in a pile at the top of the table, and spoons were placed in another pile in the middle of the table. I watched as Bren struggled before she gave up and started laying the table. The look of surprise on her face was priceless when she reached where Onyx was sitting. She laid the spoons in front of him with a serviette.

"Thanks, sweetie," he said to her. Her head shot up in surprise at his thanks.

"Um, you're welcome," she whispered before continuing with her job.

When she was finished, she sat down next to me, and I slipped my arm around her shoulders and squeezed her. My breath stopped briefly as she leaned her head slightly on my shoulder before sitting back up.

Ellie had not been as shy and was standing next to Dragon, chattering away, helping him butter the toast.

I couldn't wait until Bren was as comfortable, but I understood that she had been hurt much in her short life, whereas Ellie had been protected by both her and Ben.

Draco brought the soup to the table and started spooning it out and passing bowls around.

There was silence as everyone ate. I was finishing and was wondering what was happening that afternoon or if the plans had changed.

"What's happening this afternoon?" I asked.

Draco looked up, "We have a meeting with Reaper to go over what can be done about the gang infiltrating the village and corrupting it. Avy and Noni are coming to the meeting, and then I think you are all heading to the next town to buy the girls some clothes."

"Oh, we don't need clothes. I can wash what we have," Bren said quickly.

Rogue laid his hand gently over Bren's, "Bren honey, you have to let Noni take you shopping. My sister goes into withdrawals if she doesn't go at least once a week. And then, man, is she a bear to live with," he rolled his eyes to the ceiling during this last comment.

I sniggered a little, thinking I needed to tell Noni what Rogue had just told the girls because I knew for a fact that it was a lie. Noni hated shopping.

"Plus, if you don't go shopping, what will we do with all these gift cards we got you," Dragon said with a smile as each of the guys reached into a pocket and laid a gift card in front of the girls. Soon they each have a pile for different stores.

Ellie's eyes are just about popping out of her head. Bren, though, my poor girl, promptly burst into tears and threw herself at Dragon.

I have to hand it to him. He didn't flinch at Bren's tears and pulled her in for a tight hug before kissing the top of her head.

Putting her back on her feet, he took his serviette and dried her face. "Enjoy your shopping, sweet girl. And make sure Noni and Avy take you for ice cream after, okay?"

She nods, giving him a beaming smile that lights up her entire face, before sitting back down next to me to start looking through all her gift cards.

I looked around the table at these battle-hardened men, their faces soft as they watched the girls and listened to their excited chatter.

Surrounded by the sounds of happy girls chatting and the deep tones of the men as they talked, it was the most contented I had been in a long time.

CHAPTER 13

REAPER

I'd hated leaving Abby in my bed. I had planned on waking her, but when Sam knocked on our door at 5:30 a.m. I knew I didn't have the time.

Slipping out of bed, I got dressed, grabbed my gym bag and jogged downstairs to find them all waiting on me.

"Thought we'd have to send out a search party if you were any longer," Draco grinned, and I flipped him off and sat to put my boots on.

Dragon tsked at me, "Only home for two weeks, and he's getting soft already."

I narrowed my eyes at him as I stood and walked past him, punching him in the shoulder, "I'll show you, soft. You and me are first in the ring."

"Whatever you say, Pres," he snapped a salute at me.

"Fucker," I muttered, going to my bike.

"Who's taking the lads?" I questioned.

"Mum is," Draco replied just as Aunt Maggie and Bella walked out the door towards the garage.

Seeing that they were ready to leave, I motioned to my boys, and we started our bikes.

I looked over at Draco and saw a huge grin on his face before it disappeared behind the visor of his helmet.

We waited for Aunt Maggie to pull out of the garage before following. There was nothing quite like riding with your brothers, knowing that if anything were to happen, they'd be there to back you up.

Following Aunt Maggie behind the café to the staff parking lot, we backed our bikes in and dismounted while we waited for the lads to get out of her car.

Draco started walking to the car to help his mum out, but Ben beat him to it and opened her door for her. She said something to him as she got out, earning her a big smile at whatever she said. Then, reaching into her shoulder bag, she pulled out a protein shake and handed it to him.

As we approached, we heard him say softly, "Thanks, Aunt Maggie."

Patting his cheek gently, she answered, "No problem, baby. When you're finished at the gym, make sure you come over for breakfast. We'll get you fighting fit in no time."

That sounded like a good plan to me, "We'll all be over for breakfast Aunt Mags. Can you reserve the two tables in the family corner?"

My aunt nodded, "Of course. Now before you go, can some of you grab today's bread from Noni for me and bring it to the cafe? It will be ready by now. How that girl starts her day at three in the morning is beyond me. If you get it now, it will save Bella and me from going over. I'm not keen on having her out with all that's going on."

Rogue, Dragon, and Alec headed over the road to collect the bread from Sticky Tricky Bakery, the MC bakery that Noni ran, and the rest of us headed down the road to the gym, which was only four doors down.

It wasn't open yet by the looks of it, but Sam pulled out a set of keys and opened up the doors before heading in and switching on the lights.

Taking a look around, I saw that it was an old-school gym with no frills about it. There was a boxing ring in the middle of the main floor with boxing bags hanging down in various areas of the gym. Off to the left were various weightlifting equipment, skipping ropes and a rowing machine.

I immediately felt at home.

Sam came back into the main gym from a closed-off area in the back with several water bottles, which he handed out.

The door behind us opened, and Dragon, Rogue and Alec walked in, taking a bottle of water from Sam.

Letting out a whoop, Dragon clapped his hands and exclaimed, "Now this is a gym. Thank fuck, I thought it would be one of those modern gyms with mirrors and shit."

We laughed at him, but I knew the rest of us were feeling just as relieved.

"Lee Masters owns the gym, and he's looking at selling. He wants to retire but won't sell to just anyone. Investors have approached him, wanting to turn it into a more modern gym, but he doesn't want that. He owns this building and the one next door, so he can hold on for a while. In the meantime, Alec and I have keys, as we like to come in early and work out. There's an honesty box in the kitchen, so if you take water, put money in so it can be replaced," Sam informed us.

I could see Rogue and Dragon looking at each other before they caught my eye.

I nodded and added it to the growing list of things to be discussed this afternoon.

We dumped our bags, and I left Draco to work with Ben. Sam and Alec had a routine outlined by the owner and got started. The rest of us took turns spotting each other.

An hour in, I turned to Dragon and pointed to the ring, "You and me," I grinned at him.

He groaned but pulled himself into the ring, bouncing slightly on his feet.

We go at it hard, we were all evenly matched when it came to fighting, and pretty soon, we are sweating hard. Dragon finally tapped out, and we got out of the ring, our chest heaving and breathing hard. Taking the towel Ben handed me, I wiped my face and turned to watch Onyx and Rogue enter the ring. We took turns pummelling each other. Once we were done, I turned to Sam and Alec, who had been watching with wide eyes.

"Your turn. Let's see where you guys are in your training."

They nodded and got into the ropes. Draco made sure their headgear, mouth guards and gloves were on and secured.

We hadn't bothered with the safety equipment. Our training was beyond that.

Rogue was answering Ben's questions, and I could see how eager he was to get started.

Clasping his shoulder in my hand, I said, "Soon, Ben. First, we need to get your weight up and build some muscle. Follow the schedule Draco set out. We will start on some basic self-defence tomorrow morning."

He shot me an animated grin and nodded.

Sam and Alec were well-matched, and I could see they regularly boxed together. They are listening to the instructions that Draco was giving them.

While we were watching them, we heard the door open behind us. Turning at the sound, I watched as an older man walked in. He was stocky, with broad shoulders and a craggy face. His nose looked like it had been broken several times. I could tell he used to be a powerhouse just by how he carried himself. Following behind him was a young girl, probably about fifteen or sixteen. She was about five foot nine, with broad, muscular shoulders and strong arms. Her light brown hair was cut short except for her fringe, which flopped over her right eye. She was kitted out in workout gear, carrying a massive duffle over her shoulder.

Her head lifted as she came closer and pulled out her earphones. She watched the match a little before her eyes roamed over the rest of us, her eyebrows raised.

The older man approached, holding out his hand, "Lee Masters, this is my granddaughter, Carly."

Shaking his hand, I introduced myself, "Kane Crow or Reaper, these are my brothers Draco in the ring with Sam and Alec, Dragon, Onyx, Rogue. And this is Ben."

He shook our hands, "You Shep's son?" he asked.

I nodded, "Yeah, and the others belong to Dog, Thor and Gunny,"

"I was sorry to hear about your dad. I hope you are going to sort this village out. It could do with a clean up."

I grinned at him, "That's the plan."

"Let me know if you need an alibi. I will happily give you one if it means our families go back to being safe," he commented while continuing to watch Draco and the boys in the ring.

"You boys know what you are doing by the looks of it. I wouldn't mind if you worked with my granddaughter."

The girl let out a little hiss, her cheeks brightening in embarrassment, "Grandpa!"

"What?" he questioned. "Having a different perspective on your training is good for you."

"But I'm not as good as them," she muttered, her eyes downcast.

The old man's gaze softened as he looked at his granddaughter, "Honey, you are. You just need some confidence, and I think they can help you with that."

Carly bit her lip before looking up at me with clear blue eyes, her face still uncertain. "Okay, but if you think I'm rubbish, you have to say because I don't want to waste anyone's time. I'm happy to help Grandpa out in the gym."

Dragon whistled to grab Draco's attention.

"Hey Draco, I have another trainee for you," Dragon rumbled.

Draco, Sam, and Alec stopped and turned to us, they were sweating hard, and their chests were heaving. Draco had worked them pretty hard. We needed to know what they could do to train them in other areas.

Sam grinned when he saw who was standing next to me, "Hey Carly, you're finally going to work with us."

Carly nodded shyly, "Only if they say I'm good enough, though," she pointed at me over her shoulder. "I don't want to waste anyone's time."

Alec laughed, "Girl, you're way better than us. We've watched you train with Lee. That's why we always ask if you want to join us. We wouldn't mind learning some of the martial arts that you know."

I was happy that the lads didn't have a problem training with a girl. I was interested to see what she could do. Dragon was helping her wrap her hands. Once she was suited up and had her mouth guard in, Sam pulled her up into the ring before getting out.

"Show me your warmup," Draco said, wanting to see what her routine was.

"I've already been for a four-mile run this morning just before we arrived here. First, I need to do some stretches, and then we can start," Carly informed him.

He nodded and moved over to the ropes closest to us as we watched her go through her warm-up. She was more flexible than the boys. I mentioned this, and her grandfather told me she used to do gymnastics but now does yoga to stay flexible.

I nodded. I could see the benefit, something to think about.

Once she was ready, she nodded to Draco, who had called for headgear. I was surprised when she shook her head and replied, "I don't like wearing it. It makes me feel like I'm suffocating. Besides, if this was in the real world and I was attacked, I wouldn't be wearing headgear. I need to be able to withstand a hit. I know you aren't going to hit today, so I don't really need to wear one."

"Okay, as long as you and your grandfather are happy with that."

Both Lee and Carly nodded.

Draco got her going, and I immediately saw that she was a great fighter. He started out easy on her and then pushed harder and harder. Not once did she falter.

What was interesting to us was that she used the close combat technique we were taught in the British Army.

I arched a brow at Lee in question.

"Her father," he answered. "He was in the Army and started her training when she was three until he died when she was twelve. She has been living with me since then, and I've tried, but I don't have the experience."

We heard a laugh from Carly. Turning my attention back to the ring, I saw that Dragon had joined Draco and Carly in the ring. He must have said something to her because she smiled widely at him. Before the three of them assumed fighting positions Draco and Dragon both attacked.

There was a whistle of approval from Onyx as he, Sam, Alec, and Ben shouted their approval and encouragement.

I watched in amusement as Onyx and Rogue exchanged money. The three in the ring were slowing down, all three with smiles on their faces. When they stopped, Draco had them do a cool down, but once that was done, he picked Carly up and did a lap around the ring with her on his shoulders, singing the chorus of *We are the Champions* by Queen.

It was a good way to end our training in the gym. I arranged with Lee that we would be here every morning at 6 a.m. for training except Sundays. Dragon and Draco were happy to work with Carly. We had all been impressed with her level of experience.

After quick showers, we headed down to the café for breakfast. As we sat digging into our food, I looked around at my brothers and the young lads sitting with us.

The café had more people today than when I had been in yesterday. We'd had a couple of people nod and greet us when we walked in.

There was a change in the air. I could feel it.

"Do you think Carly would teach my sisters how to defend themselves?" Ben asked me quietly.

"You could ask her. I think it would be a good idea. If she's not comfortable doing it, then I'll do it. I want to get Bella, Avy and Noni back into training, too," I answered him.

He nodded, the tension easing from his shoulders. I ruffled his hair a bit.

"Don't worry, Ben. We'll make sure the girls are safe. It's not just you anymore. You have all of us," I motioned around the occupants sitting at the table.

We finished up, and Ben piled the plates and took them over to Bella at the counter. Sam and Alec followed with the tea and coffee cups.

I looked on in approval. Then, looking around, I saw the same approval on the faces of Draco, Onyx, Dragon, and Rogue.

Getting up, I pushed my chair back in.

"See you all back at the house for the meeting at one. I'm going with Sam to look at something, then to the hospital to see dad," I told them.

Getting nods and goodbyes, Sam and I left the café.

Alec was heading to work at the garage with Gunny, and Ben had opted to stay with Aunt Maggie and Bella to help out.

I walked down the pavement with Sam until we got to their family business at the end of the street. We carried on around the back towards what looked like a massive barn. Sam unlocked it and opened the doors before hitting the light switch.

I blinked, taking in all the furniture sitting around, some completed, some half-finished, others waiting to be oiled and polished.

Sam was standing at the door with an uncertain look. "Why did you bring me here, Sam?"

He took a deep breath and blurted out, "I want to do the carpentry and build the bar at the new clubhouse. I brought you here to show you what I've built. I can get references, and if you want an adult to be there, I can have my mentor Larry come and supervise."

I turned back to the furniture and ran my hands and eyes over them. They were beautifully made.

"You built all of this?" I asked, waving my hand around the room.

He nodded, grabbing his phone out of his pocket. He brought up photos of a stall at a fair. The picture showed him and an older man standing in front of the gazebo with woodworking pieces surrounding them.

"This is Larry and me last weekend at a country fair. We sold out. I can do this job, Reaper, and I promise if I need help, I will ask Larry to come out."

"How do I pay you? You're just a kid, so I can't imagine that you have a company set up or anything."

Sam laughed a little, "For now, jobs are going through Larry's carpentry business. I have shares in it. My jobs are paid into a savings account, and Larry takes what he needs for taxes and stuff. He and mum set it up when I started earning my own money and getting commissions. Once I hit eighteen, I'll buy Larry's company as he wants to retire. He's just waiting on me. Oh, and Grandma Kate says I should show you her dresser if you are unsure about me doing the job."

I laughed out loud at this comment before holding my hand out and shaking Sam's hand.

"The job is yours. Let me know what you need. I also want a table built for the meeting room."

"Come and look over here. I have some rough sketches drawn. I overheard Noni and Avy discussing the logos one day, and I took a peek at them. I drew this that night. What do you think?" He asked, flipping over a page on the drawing board in the corner.

"It's perfect," I replied as my eyes slowly wandered over the page. The table was oval-shaped and in the centre was our logo of a crow sitting on a pile of bones, with Crow MC at the top and our chapter name and location at the bottom.

"Can you carve the logo, or do you have someone else that can do it?" I asked.

"I can do it. I just need your approval. I'll have to build the table in the meeting room. The door isn't big enough for me to get a table this size through. Once it's in there, it isn't moving. These are the chairs I have planned to go with the table," Sam said, walking over to the back of the room and pulling a dust cover from a finished chair.

I stand in shock as I look at the chair. There had been real thought put into it. It was almost throne-like, the seat was done in red leather, and the arms of the chair had crows in various stages of flight along the arm ending in what looked like claws where it cured down. Walking around it, the back had our logo carved into it. It would be beautiful when the chairs were pushed under the table. Our MC logo was everywhere.

"Sam, I don't know what to say. This is fucking amazing. How did you have this ready for me to look at today? I've only been back for two weeks."

He flushed slightly before saying, "I overheard your dad and Dog arguing about a month ago just after I found the logo. Dog wanted you to come home, and Shep didn't want you to come home until you were ready. All my life, I've heard of you all and seen the photos and the pride on their faces when they spoke of you. I had a feeling that, eventually, someone would tell you all what was happening here.

"So, I thought I would start building, that way I'd have something to show you when you got home. I wasn't expecting you all to be home so soon. I'm sorry Grandpa had to be hurt, but I'm glad you are all home now. I've been worried about mum going out on jobs alone, so I've been going with her. Otherwise, all the chairs would have been done by now."

I pulled him into a hard hug before releasing him, gripping his shoulders.

"You make me proud, Sam. You're a great lad. Your mum did a fantastic job with you. I'd be proud to sit on that chair at the table you build for us. And maybe one day you can join us at that table," I smiled at him.

Sam grinned at me, pride clear on his face.

He showed me a few other pieces before I had to leave to see my dad. I made sure he was okay by himself. He assured me he was and that he would catch a lift home later with Gunny and Alec.

Leaving, I went back to the café and my bike. My mind was whirling as I rode to the hospital.

There had been a slight change during the night when dad seemed to wake slightly but then went straight back to sleep. We were hoping this meant he was on the road to improvement.

My day went from good to great as I stepped into the kitchen just as everyone finished lunch and watched my woman laugh with my brothers and the little girls tucked in close to her.

I was impatient to get rid of these drug dealers as they took away the time I should be spending wooing my woman.

Walking straight to her, tilting her head back slightly, I bent and kissed her on her lips. Her eyes widened with surprise until she realised who it was, and then I got another kiss.

Joining them at the table, I took a bowl of soup while listening to the conversation. It felt good to be home.

The rest of the family slowly made their way into the kitchen, and everyone, including mum, was waiting when one o'clock rolled around.

Standing up, I said, "Right, all adults, to the main dining room for the meeting."

Looking at Bella, Bren, Ellie, and Ben, "If you guys can clean up, we won't be more than an hour. I know the ladies have shopping planned for this afternoon."

I pulled Abby up from her chair and led the way into the main dining room.

She protested as we entered the room, "I don't need to be here, Kane. I can help the kids clean."

Looking at her, I pulled out a chair and said, "Babe, you and I are happening. Women will be part of our meetings. You all own and run businesses in the village. You have a unique way of looking at things that we as men don't."

I smiled as a glow lit her eyes after my speech. "Okay." She nodded and sat down in the chair I held for her.

Once we were all seated, I looked around the table. Abby was in the chair to my right, with Draco on my left. The rest had found seats similar to how we sat at the dinner table, except for the parents taking up the bottom of the table.

"Before the meeting starts, I want to tick a few boxes. Avy, can you take notes in the first half, as it will be mostly business? Dragon, if you can do the second half if notes are needed."

I got affirmative nods from both of them, and Avy pulled a computer from her backpack, getting ready to take notes.

"First, are all of you happy with resurrecting the MC?"

There were resounding yesses from around the table.

"Okay then, now that's settled, I want to ask if the originals want places at the table as officers or are you staying retired?"

"We are happy to stay retired," Dog answered. "But if you need us, we're here and would like to continue attending meetings."

I got nods from all the originals, mum and Maggie.

"Right now, that's cleared up. Avy and Noni have something for the rest of you," I motion to my brothers around the table.

Noni got a box from the corner of the room and thumped it down on the table, pulling our new colours from the boxes. She handed each one down to me, where I stood at the top of the table.

First were the new colours for our originals. I picked up the boxes that held their colours and approached Dog, Gunny and Thor.

"I know you have your original cuts, but we wanted you to be part of the new MC, so we got these made for you."

I handed them each a box, and they slowly pulled their new colours out and held them up. I swore Gunny had a tear in his eye as he saw the back patch with a crow on a pile of bones with Crow MC on the top rocker and our village Feannag Chapter New Forest and Original on the bottom rocker. Only those who started or grew up in the MC would have the original, and any new members would only have our chapter.

I handed mum two boxes, one containing dad's cut and one containing her new one. Next, I gave Dog, Aunt Maggie's box, and he pulled it out before turning to her.

"Maggie love, would you do me the honour… again," he grinned at her.

She laughed at him, turning her back as he slipped it on. Dog raised his eyes, noticing the change on her vest, before slanting his eyes to Noni in question.

She sighed and explained, "Kane gave us a choice. We could have *property of* on the back if we wanted. He didn't care. We decided that while we didn't want it blazoned across the back, we still wanted it added. Aunt Maggie, if you turn around, please."

Maggie turned, and on the top left-hand side was a patch that read, *Property of Dog*.

"I like it," Aunt Maggie smiled.

Mum pulled hers out of her box. I stood and took it from her. "Let me, mum."

I settled her new property vest on her shoulders, and she turned round with a big smile on her face. "Your dad will be over the moon when he wakes up. I will wear it from now on when I'm out and about. Not only will it be the first thing he sees when he wakes, but the rest of the village will realise you are back and serious about cleaning up."

Going back to my seat, I pulled the rest of the boxes towards me and opened the one on top, seeing my sister's name. I made my way around to her and put it on her.

She grinned, stroking her hand down her name with the *Property of Crows MC* under it.

I handed Thor the box with Noni's property patch in, and we watched as he helped her. His face was alight with pride as he settled it on her shoulders before pressing a kiss to her forehead.

Opening the next box, I saw that it was Draco's. There was an additional clear plastic bag with what I could see was our position. I knew they all expected me to be President, but I still felt like I needed to ask, as any of my brothers could do the job.

Looking around the table, I meet every one of my brothers' eyes, "Before I continue, I want to ask for a vote for the President's position. Just because it was my dad's does not mean it should automatically come to me. I would be honoured to follow any of you, so I'm putting forward that we vote for the President posit ….."

I didn't finish before Dragon said, "I vote for Reaper to be president."

"Second," Draco replied.

"Third," Onyx shouted out.

"Sorry brother, guess you're it," Draco grinned at me.

I shook my head at him, "If that's the case, then I put you forward as VP."

184

There are resounding ayes around the table. I grinned and handed him his cut and VP patch.

"The following officer's positions will be as follows if anyone has any complaints… tough shit. Suck it up," I grinned at the three remaining men.

"Onyx, you're Sergeant at Arms, Rogue's Road Captain. Plan a run soon, brother. We need to be seen. Dragon's the Treasurer, and you will work with Noni and Avy. Any questions?"

Getting resounding no all around, I hit the table with my hand.

"Right onto the next thing, buying the land next door and the gym."

I looked at Noni and Avy as they had all the business financials.

"Where are we on money, and can we afford both? We all have savings we can add to the kitty."

Noni and Avy had big grins on their faces, as did the rest of the Originals. I was guessing the books looked good by the looks on their faces.

Avy cleared her throat, "I think we need to bring Bella in for this next round. In fact, she needs to be part of these meetings as, without her, none of what we have in the coffers would be there."

I nodded. Avy got up and went to get Bella. I wondered what was going on but had learnt to trust my sister and Noni when it came to business. They had far more experience than us.

We heard Bella arguing with Avy as they approached the dining room. "I don't need to be there, Avy. You can tell them anything they need to know."

"Girl, you listen to me. You made it possible for them to buy these properties, so you can bloody well come in and take the praise."

"I don't need praise, Avy. I do it for fun," Bella muttered.

"And I don't care. Get your behind into that dining room before I make you."

"Yeah, you and whose army? I'm bigger than you."

There was a squeal, and the door slammed open as Avy propelled Bella into the room with her shoulder shoved into Bella's stomach.

"You're such a bully," Bella groaned, rubbing her stomach.

"And you're a brat, but I love you anyway," Avy laughed.

There were chuckles around the table as the two of them sat down, still shoving at each other.

I cleared my throat, and their eyes swung to me.

"If you two are finished, shall we get on?"

Bella's face flushed, "Sorry."

I smiled at my young cousin, "No worries, sweets. Avy, what have you got for us?"

"Three million."

There was silence before we all started talking at once.

"Where the fuck did that come from?" I exclaimed.

Avy, Noni and Bella had huge grins on their faces. The only ones of the Originals not looking surprised were mum and Aunt Maggie.

"Well, our little Bella has a thing for the stock market. Tell him, Bella."

"I like numbers. When I was fourteen, someone came to the school to discuss finances. One of the things discussed was stock markets. I was intrigued and wanted to try to play them. I had my pocket money saved but no account, so I asked Avy if she would open an account with me. Not mum because she would have said no."

Aunt Maggie nodded her head in agreement with this comment.

"Anyway, I tried it with some of my money and lost it. But I didn't give up and carried on until I figured out what to do. Every time I won, I put it aside in a savings account. Before I knew it, I had five thousand pounds saved, so I took half and used that. And that's how I started. I never used all my money, just some. Avy and Noni saw what I was doing and gave me money. I warned them I didn't always make a profit, but they still believed in me. They opened a company, but of course, I'm not old enough yet to be added, but it's all legal, with a contract. I get added at eighteen. So yeah, that's how we made money," she shrugged like it was no big deal.

We sat there with our mouths agape at what she had just told us. Our sixteen-year-old sister and cousin had, over the last three years, accumulated the MC enough money to buy a new business and buy the property next door.

"Why are you working in the café if you can do all this?" I asked.

Bella shrugged and looked at me like I was nuts, "Because mum needs reliable staff."

Well, there's not much I can say about that. I felt slightly chastised.

"So, Bells, if I give you some money can you grow it for me," Onyx asked.

"Sure, I can discuss it with you, but you'll have to sign a contract understanding that you may lose it all and you have to pay our company ten per cent of what we make you. I don't work for free," Bella replied.

I grinned at Onyx and Draco, taunting, "Guess we know who got all the brains."

After much laughter, we settled down to business. Now that we knew the coffers were looking good, I gave the go-ahead for mum and Draco to go next door and make an offer on the farm. And for Dragon and Rogue to speak to Lee Masters about buying the gym and the property next door. Avy suggested we look into turning it into a hairdresser and spa, as there was nothing in our village, and everyone had to drive to the next town for that.

Once we were done with business, the women stood up to leave. I pulled Abby down for a kiss. She had been quiet throughout the meeting, and I wondered what she thought. I waited until the door closed behind them before turning to the men at the table.

"Right, let's get busy planning to clean our village. I have a woman to romance, and this shit is cutting into my time with her."

CHAPTER 14

ABBY

I'd been quiet throughout the meeting. I watched the dynamic between the main five and how the men viewed Kane as the automatic leader. It seemed ingrained. I imagined it had been like that from childhood. They naturally fell into a rhythm that suited each of their personalities. Kane's personality was to watch and see if a situation resolved itself. If it didn't, then he would step in and end it.

Draco was a hot head, and he would jump in without thought. They evened each other out, each one there to either push or pull the other back, depending on the situation.

The other three were content to follow them. Onyx gave off a slightly mysterious air, and he had a coldness. I could imagine he would be formidable in a fight. He was very focused and could hold anyone captive with his dark gaze. The only softness I had ever seen in him was with his mum, Kate, Bella, Noni, and Avy.

Rogue was just as his name portrayed him, slightly mischievous with a restlessness about him. I could see why they had made him Road Captain. I imagined he needed the space. He was always moving, and his knee hadn't stopped bouncing the whole meeting.

Other than Kane, Dragon was the one I found the easiest to be around. He had a protectiveness about him that extended to his brothers and the rest of the family. I think that was why the girls were so drawn to him. They knew he wouldn't let anything happen to them while they were with him.

We had left them planning a recon mission, and I was a little apprehensive about what they would face. However, I had to keep reminding myself that they had done this for a living before retiring from the military.

After a kiss that had left me wanting more, I'd left the meeting with the rest of the women stopping off in the now spotless kitchen to pick up the girls and their vouchers.

Piling into Avy's car, she had a Ford Transit Tourneo that she used for stock and carrying punters who had too much to drink home after closing.

I got into the back seat with Bren and Ellie. Queen blasted through the speakers as she started the car. I grinned and started singing along with *Bohemian Rhapsody* as we pulled out of the drive and onto the main road. We sang all the way to the next town and the shopping centre.

Out of the corner of my eye, I saw Bren give a little shoulder shimmy, and pretty soon, she was boogieing along with Ellie and me in the back seat.

I loved seeing them let loose a little and be silly with us.

Shopping with girls was an experience. I was used to shopping with Sam, and usually, it was a quick in and out, but with the girls needing everything, it took a long time. Ellie loved it, but Bren checked every price and worked out the most cost-effective way to spend their vouchers.

I could see Ellie was about to have a meltdown when Bren made her put another cute top down because she could have three plain ones for the same price as the one with a sparkly butterfly print on it.

Stepping up to the girls, I put an arm around each of their shoulders.

"Why don't we have Avy and Ellie go and look at the clothes for Ellie's age, and you and I hit the teen stuff, Bren? Then, we'll head over to the men's and grab Ben some stuff. How's that sound?" I asked.

Avy nodded in agreement, "Yeah, let's do that and then we'll go grab a coffee or milkshake."

I could see the indecision on Bren's face as she looked at Ellie and then to the top she wanted. Finally, her eyes welled with tears, and she agreed, allowing Avy to take Ellie's hand.

"I'm sorry," Bren whispered. "It's just that she would have got more wear out of the three tops than one pretty one."

I hugged her and kissed the top of her head, "I know, honey, but today, I don't want you to worry about money. You get what you need, and let us worry about the balance after your vouchers are gone."

"Okay." She nodded, drying her face on the tissue I handed her.

"Hey Bren," we hear Noni call out, "Come look at these boots. I think they will be great when you go on a bike."

Bren's eyes widened. "You really think that someone will take me for a ride?"

"Absolutely, they will, and if one of the guys can't, then either Avy or I will. We both ride."

There was a look of awe on Bren's face as she looked at Noni.

"Wow, you ride?"

"I sure do. I even have a bike at the manor. I'll show it to you when we get home. You can ride too when you're old enough to get your licence."

I grinned as Bren started peppering Noni with questions, not noticing when we started loading our baskets with stuff for her to try on.

Before long, we were heading over to the men's section to get Ben's clothing, including boots and trainers.

After finishing up, we met Avy and Ellie by the doors. Ellie was bouncing on the tips of her new pink trainers. She had a new outfit that included a pretty top with sparkles on the front.

Bren smiled at her sister, "You look pretty, Els. I like your new trainers."

Ellie squealed and hugged Bren before moving to me and then to Noni. Then, throwing back her head, she shouted, making us all laugh, "Best day ever!"

We headed over to a local café that served coffee and milkshakes. Deciding that we had nearly everything, I said I needed to stop at the local Savers to pick up some monthly items. Bren hadn't said anything, but I assumed she would need stuff for her period. I didn't want to make a big deal out of it, so when I got in the door, I grabbed a basket. Casually saying as I chucked a box of tampons in, "Bren, if you need anything just chuck it in the basket, okay."

Getting a nod, she added what she needed. I took the basket over to the tills to pay, meeting them back outside. We headed back to the car in the parking lot, jumped in and headed back home.

CHAPTER 15

REAPER

As soon as the door closed behind the women leaving for the girls' shopping trip, I turned to the men in the room.

"What do we know about the ACES so far? Gunny, you and Thor, and Dog need to point us in the right direction."

"So far, this is what we have," Dog said, standing and walking to a whiteboard hidden in the corner. He pulled it out. It showed a map of the village.

"We know they are cooking meth somewhere around here. But their main drugs come up from the coast through the villages as they know the police don't have the manpower to do anything about it. Then through to London. They are transported via caravans and motorhomes. They set it up as a family on holiday, which is why they are hitting schools not just for distribution but also to provide cover.

"They are clever. They only do the runs during the main camping season, from

March through September. That's how they have kept off the radar for so long. The problem with them using kids for distribution and cover is that they can't help but get cocky. That's how this has all blown up. Not sure how we can stop the transport, but we can slow down their production by getting rid of where they are cooking meth."

"I can help with the cooking sites," Gunny said gruffly.

Raising an eyebrow, I study him. "Yeah?"

Gunny nodded, pulling on his beard. By the stares Dog and Thor were giving him, they didn't know what information he had.

"Up until six months ago, I had someone on the inside, but I've checked the intel, and they are still using the sites for cooking. They are all within twenty miles of here."

Pulling a map from his back pocket, he laid it on the table and opened it up. The map was marked with fifteen red dots, all close to the manor.

Studying the map, I noticed they seemed to be old farms or undeveloped industrial areas.

"How do you know the person who gave you this won't give you up?"

He surprised us with the answer.

"Because it's Beverly, Alec's mother. She came to me when Alec was ten and getting into trouble he shouldn't be. She asked if he could come to the workshop after school and start working. The boy has always been good at mechanics. I was wary at first but agreed. Over the years, we've got to know each other. She got hooked on drugs when she was twenty-one and working in London. Alec's mother was a Personal Assistant to a big wig in the city. She found herself in the position of mistress, and he had her set up in a flat in London but kept her high most of the time. She finds out she's pregnant at twenty-five and refuses to have an abortion, so he kicks her out. So she came back here to where she grew up.

"Kept clean for three years before he found her again. Unfortunately, she doesn't stay clean this time, and he uses her as a prostitute for his important clients. She kept it from Alec for as long as she could, but when his father started making noises about spending time with him and with Alec constantly in trouble, she knew she had to get him off the estate.

"I was friends with her father, so she came to me. Alec has been living in the back room of the garage since then, or he's here with us. Beverly wanted out, her clientele had been getting rougher and rougher, and a couple of the girls had been killed.

"She's a strong woman. When the other girls were killed, she started weaning herself off the drugs, getting the information she could and passing it on to me. Hence the map. I got her out six months ago. Paying for a new name and identification, I got her into rehab to get the care she needed. I have her stashed in a place up north until she's completely clean and can come home.

"Before you ask, Alec is aware of what's going on. He always has been. The two of them don't keep secrets anymore. It's too important to his safety. Once I knew what was going on, I got him papers and gave him my name. As far as his father is aware, he died in an accident on the estate when he was ten. The problem we're going to have is that the sperm donor has moved up in society and is now a member of parliament."

There was silence as we all processed what was being said, only broken by Thor letting loose and punching Gunny straight in the jaw.

"What the fuck?" Gunny groaned, rubbing his chin where the punch had landed.

"You've been doing this alone for years, Gunny. We're your brothers, for fuck's sake. You come to us, and you don't do it alone. That's how Shep ended up in the hospital. Jesus, I'm fucking glad the boys are home. Maybe they can knock some sense into all you stupid old fucks. We work better as a team. We all thought Alec was yours, but you didn't want him to know."

"He may not be mine by birth, but he's my boy all the same," Gunny muttered, still rubbing his face.

"Jesus fuck, you still hit hard, Thor. I think you knocked a tooth loose."

I banged on the table, "All right, boys, if you are finished? If you aren't, you can take this to the ring tomorrow morning."

Getting chuckles from around the table, I stand up and look around.

"We'll need to do some recon tonight, and we'll need supplies."

"We've got you covered. Well, Noni's ex-father-in-law has you covered," Thor grumbled, still annoyed.

"What do you mean Noni's ex-in-law has us covered?" Rogue interjected. "I thought her ex is in prison for life?"

"He is, but he still keeps in contact with Noni. You know he forced the divorce. Not many know that his dad still has a finger in a few pies. One of them is guns. When we saw how things were going, Noni went and spoke to him and got a few supplies, some I think you'll be surprised at," Dog grinned happily.

"Okay, so where do we find this treasure trove?" I asked.

Gunny slid a key across the table at me, "Follow the path past the barn to the old abattoir at the end of the road. It looks like it's falling down, but a bunker under the old office floor is still completely intact. We'll come and show you because it's hidden. Sam found it by accident one day. We think it was used during the War to hide allies or spies. When we opened it up, there was an old bed, table, and chair in there."

Standing, we all headed out. When we passed through the kitchen, I saw Ben sitting at the table with Mum and Aunt Kate helping them peel and chop vegetables for what I assumed was going to be our supper. He had another shake close to hand. I squeezed his shoulder as I walked past and got a smile in reply.

We made short work of getting to the old abattoir. It looked like it was falling apart, Gunny entered the doorway, and we could see some of the repairs that had been made but not many. From a distance, it still looked derelict. He went to the far corner and pressed down on one of the panels. Draco jumped as the floor moved where he was standing, making the rest of us laugh.

"Dicks," he muttered, narrowing his eyes at us.

Bending, I inserted the key in the lock, turned it, and pulled up the hatch door to find myself looking at a set of steps. Gunny handed me a torch, "You'll find a light switch when you get to the bottom. We had Abby's dad update the wiring before he passed away. Nobody but us knows this is here. The women didn't want to know. Plausible deniability."

Nodding, I went down the steps until I saw the light switch. Flicking it on, I whistled when I saw the cache they had hidden down there. Boxes upon boxes of ammunition, guns, crossbows, and knives.

The others had followed me down. It was getting a little cramped.

Dragon was turning in circles, trying to get a good look at everything. He moved over to one of the boxes, lifted the lid, and made a happy noise in his throat.

Walking over, I saw the explosives. Clamping him on the shoulder, I let our demolition guy enjoy the view.

"This looks like military issue," Draco muttered, picking up a handgun to inspect it.

"Ask no questions, and I tell you no lies," Thor grinned at him.

"I don't care where it comes from if it is used to protect our family," I replied. "I have girls now. No fucker's coming near them."

There's a loud shout of agreement from the men around me.

We spend a happy hour going through everything and sorting it for easier access.

I grab the night vision goggles, a bullet-proof vest, a handgun, and a couple of knives.

I turned to the others, "Suit up with what you think you'll need. We'll be splitting up for recon tonight Gunny with me, Draco and Thor, Rogue and Dog, and Onyx and Dragon. And remember, recon only for tonight. Tomorrow, we'll make a plan."

They all nodded and grabbed what they needed, putting them into the black backpacks that were hanging on the wall behind them. We left the cellar, locked it, and headed back to the house. The women were back from shopping. We headed into the house filled with laughter, noise, and the smell of curry.

My stomach growled. I'd missed home-cooked meals so much.

"Ace, Mum's curry," Onyx whooped as he pushed and shoved to get past us to the pot his mum was stirring.

We laughed as she slapped him when he tried to get a taste.

I made for my woman, who was leaning against the counter, a bottle of beer in her hand, watching everyone. I leaned down and caught her lips in a hard kiss, tasting the beer on her tongue.

I hummed in approval as my lips left hers. Taking Abby's beer from her hand, I take a swig. It was good. I turned it, looked at the label, and saw it was made locally. I handed it back to her.

I watched Onyx as he tried again to sneak some food, only to get another slap with the dish towel. The kids were laughing, and I knew he was hamming it up for them.

Feeling content, I leaned against the counter with Abby wrapping my arm tight around her shoulder. Watching our family and laughing at their silliness.

CHAPTER 16

ABBY

It was ten o'clock when the men had all just left to go and do recon on the sites that Gunny and Beverly pinpointed. To say I was concerned was an understatement. I had to keep reminding myself that they had done far more dangerous things during their time in the military. It would be like a walk in the park for them.

It had been a bit of a shock finding out who Alec's father was. It meant that Alec was Sam's uncle, as Alec's father was Sam's grandfather. I needed to speak to Katie and Maggie for advice on how to tell Alec and Sam they were related.

Like most of the family, I had always assumed Gunny was Alec's father. They had a close relationship and did most things together.

I left Bren and Ellie's room after getting them settled and their new clothes packed away. Ben had decided to sleep in the room with Sam and Alec. I headed there next. The door was partially open. Knocking on it, I heard Sam call out, "Come in."

Pushing it open, I looked in to see the three of them in bed, each with a book, reading.

"You boys all good for the night?"

"Yeah, we're good, mum. What time do you expect Reaper and them back tonight?"

"I'm not sure, but probably not until early morning."

"Cool, it's Saturday tomorrow. Can you drop us at the gym at six? I don't think Draco will be up to take us if they're coming in late."

"Yeah, of course, I'll set the alarm. Although I'm sure they will be up to take you in. Either way, I need to go to the house and check on things anyway, as we haven't been there for a couple of days."

"Okay. Mum, are we moving in here permanently?"

Sighing, I walked into the room and sat on his bed, very aware that we had two other boys in the room listening to our conversation, even if they were pretending not to while focusing on whatever they were reading.

"I don't know, Sam. Kane and I haven't had much time to talk. The last few days have been full-on. I'm not denying there is something there, but I will speak to you before I make any decisions. Will it be a problem for you if we move here?" I asked him.

I got a wide grin at my question, "No, it's not a problem for me. I would prefer it. Alec lives here full-time now, and with Ben and the girls moving in, I think it would be good. I still want to keep my woodwork shop, though. But I thought if we lived here, we could strip everything out of the house, redo it, and rent it out to get some extra income?"

I mulled this over, it was a good plan, but I needed to speak to Kane first. I knew we could still move in here even if Kane and I didn't work out. Katie had offered several times since dad had passed away.

"Let me speak to Kane first, but it is a good idea."

Getting up to leave, I said, "Night, boys, lights out in an hour."

I got three *goodnights*.

Just as I was about to close the door, Alec stopped me, "Leave the door ajar, Mamma A. Ben likes to be able to hear the girls if they need him."

Nodding, I did that before heading for a shower. I find Avy sitting on the bed when I open Kane's door, doing something on her phone.

"Kids all good?" she asked.

"Yeah, they're good. What's up, hun," I asked while I headed to the dresser and grabbed trackie bottoms and a T-shirt intending to head to the shower.

"We're going to meet in the family room and wait for the guys. Aunt Kate and Aunt Maggie have opened up the wine and told me to come to get you," Avy replied.

"Okay, give me ten minutes to grab a shower, and I'll be down," I confirm, heading into the bathroom.

Ten minutes later, I'm in the family room with some of my favourite women. Wine bottles are open, and snack boards with salami, cheese, and olives are on the coffee table. We are all dressed for comfort in leggings, trackie bottoms, and t-shirts. Even Aunt Kate was dressed for comfort, although she still looked elegant in mauve-fitted yoga pants with a matching shirt.

Taking the glass of wine she handed me, I got comfortable on the floor by her legs. Then, taking a big sip of my wine, I lean my head back on her knees and sigh.

I feel her hand run over my head, and I tilt up to look at her to find her smiling at me.

"So, sweetheart, do you want to talk about what we learned from the men after their little meeting," she questioned kindly.

I groaned, rubbing at the tension in my forehead before replying.

"I suppose I should. I don't really know if I should tell them or not that Alec is Sam's uncle. It was a bit of a shock finding out."

Thankfully the kids had all gone up when Gunny shared the news with the rest of us after dinner. He had looked straight at me when he had told us the news. I could see as soon as the penny dropped with the rest of the Oldies. I had seen Kane had questions. Gunny had offered to fill him in while they travelled, and I had agreed, so by now, Kane would know that my son's grandfather and Alec's father was the man in government who was in charge of the ACES and the cause of the drugs in this area and the cause of Kane's father being in hospital in a coma.

"Do they need to know?" Noni asked.

"Yeah, I think they do in case they are approached. I know Alec's sperm donor thinks he's dead, and I'm not sure if he even knows about Sam, as I never went to their house. When I told Todd I was pregnant, we'd only been together for six months, and he said to have an abortion.

"He didn't want anything to do with Sam. He signed his rights away as soon as he had the paperwork and disappeared. We've never had any contact. The last I saw of him was in some celebrity rag. He's married and living in the USA now. He has two girls and a son. I doubt he will be getting in contact, but I suppose forewarned is forearmed.

"I don't think there are many people left in the village who would remember who his father is other than Todd's girlfriend he had after me, but I think she moved up north somewhere."

"I'll speak to them tomorrow, and I'm sure Kane has questions too.

"Anyway, enough about me. What are you all doing here, especially you, Noni? You'll not get much sleep if you're opening the bakery tomorrow morning."

"Pshaw," she snorted, waving a hand at me with a grin. "I knew we would be up late, so I asked Marie if she would mind opening for me. She's saving for a holiday, so she was happy about the hours. Plus, I miss our girls' nights of wine and whispers. We haven't done it in months. And now that it looks like you're going to be part of the family, we can have them more often," she teasingly said.

Her happiness was catching, and I grinned back at her before asking, "Yeah, explain this Crow man thing to me, by the way. What the hell, he sees me, and I'm claimed?"

Maggie and Kate laughed at my annoyance. "Oh, my girl, let me fill you in on the Crow men and how they operate. But first, you'll need more wine for it," Maggie stated, filling my glass to the brim.

I spent the next few hours listening to Maggie and Katie tell stories about their men, and learn more about the MC and how it was started. Maggie and Katie had never been in this position before either of sitting up and worrying because their generation didn't have any issues, and the MC had nearly gone defunct.

"It was a different story for my fathers-in-law's group in the 50s and 60s. Things were wild in that era, especially in London. By the time Shep was ready to take over in the 70s, everything had calmed down, so there wasn't much need for the MC. It was only Shep, Dog, Thor, Gunny, Jones, and Roman by then. Unfortunately, we lost both

Roman and Jones in the Falklands. It hit them hard when Jones died but Roman, he was the one that hurt them the most," Katie said sadly.

"Ah, Roman," Maggie murmured, smiling softly. "He was a sweetheart, for sure. Always a kind word or a hug when you were feeling down. He was the soul that bound those men together. They weren't the same after he died. It was like a spark left them all. This is the first week I've seen that spark back in my Robert."

"You're right, Maggie. All the men seem to have a bit more pep in their step this week. Now, if only Alan would wake up, my life would be complete," Katie said.

"It's so weird hearing you call them Robert and Alan. I sometimes forget they have other names other than Shep and Dog," Noni said, grinning. She was slouched down on the couch with Avy's head on her lap. She'd fallen asleep about ten minutes ago.

"Lightweight," I said as I nudged Avy with my foot, making her grumble at me.

"Yep, the girl has never been able to hold her liquor. I better get her to bed, then head out to the hospital," Katie said, standing up.

It was nearly two o'clock, so I got up from the floor where I had been sitting and started clearing away the remnants of the last couple of hours. Taking it all into the kitchen, I helped Maggie and Noni load the dishwasher and clean up before saying goodnight as we all head up the stairs to bed.

After checking on the kids, I make short work of brushing my teeth before falling into bed with a groan, leaving the lamp on in the corner so that the room isn't in full darkness. Just as I start dozing off, I hear Kane open the door quietly.

Sitting up, I ask him, "How did it go?"

He was smiling as he came over to the bed, leaning over me, his palms cupping my face, tilting my head up as his lips landed on mine. He smelled of the night and the slight musk of a man. His kiss was long and wet. I lifted my hand and threaded my fingers through his hair tugging him closer with a moan. His mouth left mine and feathered kisses down my cheek, then towards my ear, where he nipped at my lobe.

"It was good. But coming home to you in my bed is even better," Kane growled in my ear. I clenched my thighs together as I whimpered at how his voice was turning me on.

"Kane," I whispered, my hands tugging at his hair, bringing his lips back to mine.

"Give me five minutes to shower, baby. I've been crawling around in the dirt for the last four hours. I'll be back before you know it," Kane said with a last kiss on my lips before standing.

"Or I could join you," I said, throwing the covers back and standing. I pulled my T-shirt off and threw it at him as I walked towards the bathroom. His guttural groan made me feel like the most beautiful woman on earth. I tossed him a wink and a smirk as I opened the bathroom door. I laughed out loud when I heard what sounded like boots being thrown down in the corner and, a belt hurriedly opened, then a zip being pulled down.

I started the shower just as Kane walked in, in all his naked glory. I licked my lips as I looked at him, taking the time to peruse him. Starting with his magnificent muscular legs, his thick thighs heavy with muscle. His cock, long and hard, standing upright against his belly, and my mouth watered for a taste. I raked my eyes up his flat stomach to his chest and over his broad shoulders before raising my eyes to his. Only to find him doing the same to me.

"God, you're beautiful," he muttered thickly.

Walking over to me, he took my mouth again before lifting me into the shower, pulling me close, he picked me up, my back resting against the wall. My legs tightened around his waist, and I gasped slightly as his cock hit my clit as he thrust his hips against mine. It had been a long time for me, and this man had worked me up for days. I could feel my orgasm building.

"I'm close, babe," I whispered to him.

"Birth control," he asked, pulling back to look at me.

Brushing his wet hair from his face, I smiled at him, "I'm clean and on the pill. You?"

"Well, I'm not on the pill, but I'm clean," he grinned at me. Then more seriously, he said, "I haven't been with anyone in two years, and the military checks us regularly."

"Okay," I told him.

"You're sure?" he asked.

"I'm sure," I whispered, nudging him with my hips. "Now fuck me already before I combust."

He pulled back and thrust up into me. I hissed as his cock stretched me.

He stopped when he bottomed out, waiting for me to adjust to his size. His forehead rested against mine. Opening my eyes, I saw him watching, I rocked my hips slightly, and he bit his lip and shut his eyes.

"Move, babe," I whispered.

That was the only encouragement he needed as he started to pound into me. Before long, I could feel that familiar tingle. Plunging a hand between us, I rubbed at my clit. My head was thrown back against the shower wall as I came hard.

"Wow, why did I wait so long?" I gasped.

Kane laughed softly, his head resting on my shoulder as he caught his breath. "Better than teenage sex then," he chuckled as his softening cock slipped out of me. Pressing a kiss to my neck, he gently let my legs down. Not letting me go, he held me tight in his arms until I was steady on my feet.

"Uh, yeah. I actually got to come," I laughed.

This was a first for me. I'd never had this before, and I found I loved it. There was no awkwardness, just pure happiness. I smiled as Kane grabbed the soap and loofah and began to wash me. I returned the favour, and by the time we finished, he was hard again.

Picking me up, he tossed me on the bed, followed me down, and proceeded to blow my mind by going down on me. Another first for me.

Sated, I snuggled into him and fell into a dreamless sleep. Woken only by the alarm at five-thirty. Groaning, I switched it off, flopping back down on the bed.

It was only then I noticed I was by myself in the bed, the bathroom light was on, and the door was cracked.

Kane switched off the light and came out. Seeing me awake, he came and sat on the bed, leaning over to kiss me.

"Why are you up so early?" he asked.

I snuggled back down into my pillow before answering, "I thought you'd still be asleep, so I promised the boys I would take them to the gym."

"Go back to sleep, baby. The guys and I'll take them. We're used to getting by on a little sleep."

"Okay," I said, my eyes already closing.

He tucked the covers around me before kissing my forehead and quietly left the room.

CHAPTER 17

REAPER

Leaving my room quietly, my woman asleep in my bed, I felt like the king of the world.

Opening the lad's door, I wake them up and head downstairs for coffee.

I find the others already in the kitchen, ready to head out.

I get the expected ribbing from them as I enter, knowing they don't mean anything by it.

Rogue sent a grin my way when he saw the smile on my face, "Yeah, someone had a good night."

I couldn't help but grin back at them. Knowing that I had found the woman meant for me was a great feeling.

Onyx groaned in disgust, throwing a tea towel at my face, "Fuck's sake get that goofy grin off your face."

"We're just taking the piss, Reaper. We're happy for you. She's a fantastic woman.

Who would have thought you'd be loved up and a proud dad of two boys and two girls a month ago?"

"That's the way to do it," Rogue said, nodding seriously. "No potty training, sleepless nights, or throwing up. Yeah, I reckon it's the way forward."

We laugh at him.

I shook my head, taking a drink of my coffee before answering.

"Life is good, brother. I hope mum has good news on the kid front, and we don't get hassled about keeping them. They're good kids. They just need a chance. Now, we'd be sitting pretty if we can just get rid of the ACES."

"Talking about the ACES and what we need to do. Are you open to more members in the MC?" Dragon asked.

I thought about it. We would need more men if we were to take out the organisation.

"Depends on who it is. I don't just want anyone. They have to have something to offer. Could you bring it to the table this afternoon? I want to discuss securing this place before we start anything heavy with the ACES. Draco is heading next door with Mum after training this morning. If we get the farm, we'll need to discuss securing it. It's a bigger property, so securing it won't be as easy."

I got nods from all of them. Then, hearing footsteps on the stairs, we finish our coffee.

"Who's driving the lads?"

Draco answered, "I'll take them."

We all headed outside, started our bikes, and followed Draco onto the main road. Mentally I began making lists of all that we needed to do.

The most important item was securing our home, followed by getting the barn ready to be used as a clubhouse and getting the meeting room done so that we didn't have to keep kicking everyone out of the dining room.

The bakery light was on as we drove past, and an older woman I didn't recognise was serving at the hatch. Considering the early hour, a small queue formed, waiting to be served.

Parking in front of the gym, we waited while Alec unlocked it.

Training went as expected. Things between Ben and Alec seemed to have settled down. I was happy to see Alec and Sam helping him. They would soon understand the importance of having brothers at their back.

After training, I left Dragon and Rogue to chat with Lee about buying the gym.

Draco left to pick up mum. Onyx and I headed to the hospital to check on dad. We kept hoping that he would wake soon. It was nearly three weeks, and I wondered if he would ever wake up.

Leaving the hospital a couple of hours later, we stopped at the café to grab an early lunch.

Full of fantastic food, Onyx and I headed back home for the afternoon meeting. Hopefully, Draco, Dragon, and Rogue would have news on the gym and farm.

We were all sitting around the dining table waiting on Draco so we could get this meeting started. He'd sent me a message to say he was dropping mum back in town and would be a little late getting back.

He came stomping into the dining room with a look of frustration on his face. Pulling out his chair, he sat down heavily.

"You, okay?" I ask him.

"Fuckin' hell, brother! Why are women so frustrating? How can someone so small be such a pain in the arse?"

There were snickers from around the room before Dog said, "I guess you met little Molly?"

"I not just met her, I met her bullet point questions on what we were going to do with the land, what it meant for her grandad, how we better not think that we would have anything to do with her business. Next time someone else can go."

"Did you at least secure the property?" I asked in amusement. Draco was usually unflappable. I was looking forward to meeting the woman that had managed to throw him.

"Yes, we got the farm but only because of her granddad. Anyway, it's with your mum and the lawyers now."

"Good," I replied.

Turning to the rest of them, "Right, now that Draco is back, let's talk security and new members. New members first," I nodded at Rogue to go ahead.

"I've had a couple of guys from our old units contact me wanting to join. Three we know, Hawk, Navy, and Bull. As you know, Bull is a Medic, and with things escalating, likely someone we'll need.

"The others that Hawk mentioned weren't in our units, so none of us knows them. These are my thoughts. The three we know join as full members, and the other four come in as prospects for six months.

"Just because they are ex-military doesn't mean they are a good fit. We all know that some are still arseholes. I have made them aware of the situation so they know what they are getting into. One good thing is that one of the guys that will have to prospect, William Adams, is good at computers. He's ex-intelligence. They are aware that the woman will be part of the MC meetings and don't care."

"Sounds good," I agreed. "Votes on what Rogue has just offered?"

There were ayes from around the table. Dragon, as our treasurer, made a note.

"Looks like we have new members coming in. Get Hawk to send you the prospects' information so we can check into it," I told Rogue. "When are you expecting them?"

"They're just waiting to get the okay from us, and they can all be here by the end of next week."

"Okay, let's make sure the cottages are ready so they can move right in."

Seeing that Dragon had noted that down I moved on to the next thing, security around the house.

"Onyx, have you got a list of what is needed security-wise for around the house?"

He nodded and passed a printed list around.

First on the list was getting the electric gates working again, then the cameras, and finally, the electric fencing one metre in from the main wall.

"That's the front and the sides. What about the back?"

"That's going to be more difficult because of the forest. But we can set traps as none of the family ever go in there. We need to think about fencing it all in once we have more cash flow," Onyx replied.

"Do a cost work up and bring it to the next meeting, and we'll see if we can't swing something. Take into account next door. We'll have to secure that perimeter too," I reminded him.

"Anything further?" I asked.

"Yeah, Lee Masters has agreed to sell the MC the gym. Lawyers have been notified, and papers are being drawn up as we speak. It should be ours soon," Dragon announced.

"That's great. I assume you and Rogue are still happy to run it?"

They both replied in the affirmative.

"Right, if that's all, we're done. First thing Monday, start getting the security setup. We can't hit the ACES while we're vulnerable. Back here Monday afternoon for a catch-up on where we stand."

With that, we all stood and headed out of the dining room. Finding all the women and kids in the kitchen, I looked at the clock, surprised to find it was after five. Knowing we'd be in the way, I dropped a kiss on my woman's head and ruffled the girl's hair as I walked past. I asked, "How long until supper?"

Noni looked at the clock on the wall before answering, "About another hour, we'll call you."

"Okay, where are the lads?"

"Outside playing football," Bella answered.

Grabbing the keys for the cottages from the board that held all our keys, we got our boots on.

"We'll be over at the cottages. We have more recruits coming in next week," I told them.

"Ooh, fresh meat," Noni grinned, wiggling her eyebrows lustily. Then winced when there was a muffled giggle from Bella. Luckily Ellie was oblivious.

"Sorry, I keep forgetting about little ears," Noni apologised.

Shaking my head, my eyes met Abby's, which were sparkling with amusement.

Meeting the rest of the men outside, we headed to the cottages to do inventory and see if there was anything that needed replacing or re-doing.

The cottages are pretty simple, with two bedrooms, a small kitchen, a bathroom, and a lounge, no dining area. My grandfather had updated them and re-roofed them in the 60s then my dad added bathrooms in the 80s.

They had beds, but the mattresses would be replaced. And white goods for the kitchens, including fridges, as none of them had any.

We made lists that I knew the women would go over. We had just left the last cottage when we heard Avy shouting that supper was ready.

CHAPTER 18

ABBY

The following three weeks were hectically busy. The clubhouse was re-wired and safe to be in. The bathrooms were up and running, as was the kitchen. Sam had relaid the wood floor and had roped Ben in to help. They had also built a massive bar down one side of the barn, and Dragon had hung mirrors on the wall making the space look bigger. Noni and Avy had bought a couple of sofas, a pool table, and a dartboard set up in the far corner.

The wood for the table for their meeting room had arrived, and Sam was building it on-site. To say my son had impressed everyone with his skill was an understatement. There were only a few weeks left of school holidays, so he worked overtime to finish it.

The new MC members and prospects had arrived and were settled in the cottages. I had to agree with Noni's assessment of *holy hotness*, she had whispered hoarsely as they had gotten out of their hired vehicle.

The three known to our men were Hawk, Navy, and Bull. The rest of the men would have to prospect as they had not served with Kane and the boys.

According to Avy, Blaze was fine with a capital F and a redhead.

Bond because he was clean cut, with his hair styled just right, and his clothes always on point, even if it was only jeans and a shirt. He had the most piercing blue eyes.

Cairo, who got his name because his mother was Egyptian, had dark soulful eyes and smooth caramel skin that he didn't mind showing off as he seemed to be averse to shirts. Not that any of us were complaining.

The last prospect was Skinny, who was not skinny at all but had muscles upon muscles and looked like he could happily bench press a bus. Out of the lot, he was the quietest and was the younger brother of Bull.

They all seemed like stand-up guys from my little interaction with them. A big plus was that they didn't care that women were part of the meetings.

As for Sam and me, we had all but moved into the manor.

After discussing with Kane and where we were headed, he laid it out for me by simply saying, "Babe, you're it for me. I'm going to marry you but not until I talk to your boy.

"Then we're going to get rid of the ACES. I'm going to fill your belly with as many babies as you'll give me to add to the four we already have. And we're going to live happily ever fucking after."

I still laughed when I thought about his face when I repeated his last sentence to him, "Happily ever fucking after or happily fucking ever after? I just want to be clear."

"Both," was his reply before he threw me on our bed and proceeded to fuck my brains out to make sure that I had no more questions about our happiness.

True to his word, he'd spoken to Sam and got his blessing. I had woken up one morning and had nearly taken my eye out when I had rubbed the sleep out of my eyes with the ring on my finger.

That was my man. He knew what he wanted and went about ensuring it was his. My ring was a gorgeous tiger's eye, my favourite stone, surrounded by a small ring of diamonds. He knew a traditional engagement ring wouldn't suit me because of my work, he'd found me a ring I could wear all the time, the stones were imbedded into the gold band so shouldn't get in the way of my working.

I'd showered and dressed in my usual blue jeans but added a bright red boho top and a bit of makeup, leaving my hair down. I'd driven straight to the gym, where he could be found at this time of the morning, walked straight up to him, grabbed his head, and laid a hot and heavy kiss on his lips.

"Yes," I replied before turning, nodding at the men and some women in the gym. I waved my left hand at them, flashing my ring as I left a swing to my hips and a bounce to my step as I walked out the door.

Hearing the loud whoops of laughter and teasing shouts from Kane's brothers and the rest of his men, I'd smiled and went to the café to share our news with any of the family that happened to be there at this early hour of the morning.

I found Avy, Katie, and Ellie at a table waiting for breakfast. Ellie was colouring a picture in a colouring book. Once they had seen my ring, Avy had let out a squeal which brought Maggie out of the kitchen and Bella from behind the counter.

After getting hugs from them all, we settled down, and I added my breakfast order to Avy's.

"You'd better let Noni know. She won't forgive you if you don't," Avy said with a grin.

Taking out my phone, I snapped a quick picture of my ring and sent a text to Noni.

My phone rang in the next second, making me chuckle. I was still smiling as I answered it, not that I could hear much, just lots of shouting and whooping.

Holding the phone away from my ear, I put it on speaker as we waited for Noni to calm down.

"Whoop, whoop, girl. You'll finally be family not only in spirit but in name too. I told that man he'd jinxed himself when he said he was too busy for a relationship," she cackled in glee.

I raised my eyebrows at that comment. Avy waved her hand in dismissal and explained, "It was just after he had arrived back, and we were discussing riding bikes and quality shags. Kane said he didn't foresee any shagging in his future, quality or otherwise, and Noni told him he'd jinxed himself. The next day he met you," she said.

I nodded in understanding and reminded Noni to send Bren over so we could go school uniform shopping before saying goodbye.

We'd just finished eating when Bren arrived and made her way over to us. Getting a hug from her and a quiet, "Congratulations, Mamma A."

Smiling up at her and tucking her hair behind her ear, "Thank you, baby. Are you ready to go school clothes shopping/?" I asked.

"Not really," she replied, her nose wrinkled up.

I laughed and said, "Me neither, but needs must. Are you ready to go, Ellie?"

"Yep," Ellie answered with a nod as she bounced off her chair and came over to me. We said goodbye and headed out for a morning of uniform shopping. The boys were lucky to have gotten out of it by giving me their sizes and were going to go shoe shopping with Kane later in the day.

CHAPTER 19

REAPER

I watched my woman's swaying hips snug in a fitted pair of jeans with a smirk on my lips as she bounced out of the Gym after laying a hot-as-hell kiss on me.

Congratulations were passed around, and I reckoned my back was bruised from all the back slaps.

Sam was grinning at me. We'd had a long chat regarding his mum. I had made it clear that I loved his mum, and I knew they came as a package deal, and I wanted to know where his head was at with me wanting to make it permanent.

"As long as you love and put mum first, Reaper, I'm happy with you getting married. And before you ask, I'm happy to have Ben and the girls in our family, and if you decide to add more to the four of us, that will be okay too. You'll only have me for four more years before I'm eighteen," he'd grinned at me.

I'd snorted at that comment, "Lad, if you think that just because you turn eighteen, you won't still be her baby, you have another thing coming. She'll still be checking on you and getting involved in your life when you're forty, with your own woman and kids."

I'd taken him with me to choose her ring but hadn't told him when I would propose. I'm not one for drama or public proposals. Plus, I wasn't going to give her a chance to say no, not that I thought she would.

That morning I'd woken up after a long night of making love to my woman. She was lying sprawled across our bed on her stomach, her hair in disarray over our pillows, and I'd known it was the right moment. I'd opened my bedside drawer, pulled out the ring box, and proceeded to slip the ring on her finger. It fit perfectly, and it looked right sitting there on her hand. I looked forward to her reaction and hoped I'd read her right. I didn't think she would want to make a big deal out of it.

The last few weeks had been busy, the new men had arrived, and it was good to see them. They all had bikes now and were settled into the cottages. They had fit in with no major drama, including not caring about the women being part of the MC meetings on the business, which made me feel better about them joining us.

Once they had been brought up to speed on the situation, we'd got a handle on securing all the properties owned by us, adding additional cameras to them all to include internal and external coverage.

We had gone to the extra expense of installing a ram-proof security gate on the front of the manor and another at the back entrance.

The back entrance was manned by the prospects on rotation with an intercom into a temporary guard hut that we'd set up. We'd build a better one when we had more time.

Hawk, Bull, and Draco had gone to the farm next door and seen to secure it as much as they could. While we didn't own it yet, I didn't want Molly and her grandfather to be in danger as they were our neighbours.

Because of the size of the farm, we'd opted to add an anti-climb fence around ten acres for now, as there was no way we could afford to fence in the entire farm.

According to Hawk, Molly had given Draco a mouth full regarding the fencing and had only calmed down once Bull had explained what was going on.

It seemed Draco and Molly were like oil and water. It was going to be interesting watching that unfold because, according to Bull, one minute, they looked like they were going to kill each other, and the next, they looked like they wanted to rip each other's clothes off.

We were planning a raid of all the meth labs within a forty-mile radius of us in the next two weeks. We'd been watching their routines such as they were, and it looked like they had a batch ready every two weeks for transport. We were planning to hit them two days before the transport went out.

While I knew it wasn't ideal because we didn't know the prospects. We'd had to bring them in on the raid as it meant more bodies to lay the explosives leaving Dog, Gunny, and Thor with my dad at the hospital or with the women and kids at the house.

We'd not be leaving them unarmed, all the women could shoot, and we'd been teaching the kids over the last few weeks. Rogue had spoken to a friend of his on the police force in the next town regarding the drug issue. They were so understaffed that they couldn't get a handle on it, plus there seemed to be pressure from higher up to turn a blind eye. He had said that if we could do anything about it, he'd arrange a bomb tip to come in, ensuring that all officers would be out on that call.

It was the best we could do for now. We'd be hitting six of the labs at one time, I knew this would rattle some cages, and we'd be getting backlash from it.

But that was a worry for another day. Today was a day for celebration and a welcome to the new members. I had a barbeque planned for tonight. Behind the new clubhouse, the prospects had built a barbeque area, including a spit and fire pit.

Tonight, it would just be family and close friends, but once this was over, I would see about inviting some of the village out. Maybe have a charity day. We needed to get back the community spirit that had been missing.

Our workouts finished for the day, we'd all showered and were meeting back in the main room. I was standing watching Carly and Sam train in the ring. She was a good teacher. He'd really filled out the last few weeks and was more confident.

Hawk leaned against the ropes next to me. "She's good," he commented.

"Yeah, she is. She will stay working at the Gym once we buy it."

He grunted in approval, "It's a nice thing you have going here, Reaper. I'm happy for you and appreciate you allowing us to join. It's been good to have somewhere to call home."

Seeing the others walk out of the changing rooms, I clapped him on the shoulder. "It's no hardship, man. Glad to have you. Just wish we didn't have the ACES to deal with," I said.

He shrugged, "If not them, it would be someone else. There's always someone who thinks they are bigger and better."

Clapping my hands to get everyone's attention, "Right, you fuckers, barbeque tonight. Dragon and Rogue, you're in charge of the meat. Onyx and Draco grab two prospects and get drinks and ice. The ladies are making salads and garlic bread. Hawk, that leaves you guys to set up the fires and get shit ready. Ben, Alec, and Sam, you three are with me. Apparently, you all need new shoes for school."

They all groaned in dismay. I shook my head, not looking forward to it either. "Don't moan at me. Take it up with Abby. I have my orders, so hit the showers."

Bull laughed, shaking his head as the lads went to the locker rooms, "Rather you than me, brother. Explain to me how you were free and single six weeks ago, and now you have a woman, two sons, and daughters and another cousin?"

I grinned at him before replying, "Just lucky, Bull, so fucking lucky."

That night, with my woman on my lap under a blanket by the firepit, chatting with my sister and Noni, I watched Ben, Sam, Alec, Carly, and Bella on the other side of the fire chatting about school. The lads had started working as a team and brought Carly and Bella into their little world. Bren was huddled beside Ben under a blanket, watching and listening to what they were saying. My girl was still quiet but not as fearful anymore. Her eyes, however, were straying to Alec on the regular, and my gut tightened. She was twelve, but with her upbringing, she was older than her years. And Alec, well, he was a young lad and completely oblivious to how Bren felt. I could see hurt coming her way, and it killed me.

My attention on that little scene was broken by Ellie running around like a rocket. Somebody had bought sparklers, and she was doing a pretty good job of decimating the packet.

The only thing that would have made me happier was if my dad had been sitting here with us.

CHAPTER 20

ABBY

We'd had a busy day. After taking the girl's school shopping, we'd stopped off at my house and checked on the refurb I was having done. I'd hired a local crew, and they were good. They had gutted everything and were currently replastering and re-doing the bathrooms. After that, the wiring I would do it myself.

We'd spent a couple of hours there with me going through paperwork that needed doing, paying bills, and scheduling jobs for the coming weeks.

The business was going well, and life was good. But I knew that life could change in the blink of an eye, so while it was peaceful, I would enjoy it.

Reaper had arranged for a barbeque that afternoon to welcome the new guys and celebrate our engagement. It was an afternoon and evening filled with laughter, good food, and family. The new guys had fitted in well. The kids seemed to have added a new addition to the group. Carly was a great girl, and she and Bella didn't seem to mind when Bren tagged along despite the age difference.

I'd noticed the same thing that Kane had. Her eyes would stray to Alec on a regular basis. My girl's heart was going to get bruised, and I already hurt for her. I knew what he was like. He'd lived either at my house or with Gunny for the last four years. Girls flocked to him, and he took what they offered. He was more like his brother Todd, Sam's father than he realised, I thought to myself. The only difference was that Alec didn't have a mean bone in his body.

Pressing a kiss to Kane's cheek, I whispered in his ear, "We'll be there to pick up the pieces, babe. Don't worry about it yet. It may still come to nothing."

Turning his head, he looked at me and growled out, "You may have to hold me back because that over there is trouble waiting to happen. Not sure how Gunny will feel with me kicking his boy's arse if he hurts our girl."

I laughed softly and turned my attention to Ellie, who had finally run out of energy and was curled up in Dragon's lap, fast asleep.

I went to stand but was waved back by Maggie, "Sit, honey. Dog and I'll take her to the house and settle her. You enjoy your night."

Bren watched as Dog gathered Ellie up in his arms. She stood up and said something to the others before making her way over to us.

"I'll go up to the house with them, Mamma A."

"You don't have to, honey. You can stay up a little later if you want," I assured her.

She shook her head, "No, I think I'm cramping their style," she said, tilting her head towards the group of teenagers sitting across from us. "I'm a lot younger than them. Besides, you bought me a bunch of books today, so I think I'll head up and get started on them."

"Did someone say something to you?" Reaper growled.

"Oh no, nothing like that. Please, Reaper, don't worry. I'm fine, I promise."

"Okay, baby," I said as I pulled her in for a hug and kiss goodnight.

She then bent to hug Reaper. That was not the first time she had done that, but every time he got a hug from her, it was like the sun had come out. And I knew she got just as much from the affection he gave freely to all the kids.

"Night, Reaper. Congratulations," she whispered before kissing his cheek.

"Night, baby girl, sleep tight."

"I will," she replied before heading to Maggie and Dog, who was waiting for her.

It wasn't ten minutes before the rest of the teenagers got up to go back to the house.

The men were talking about heading out and hitting a nightclub. Avy and Noni had given them a list of the best ones to go to. Draco, Onyx, and Rogue were keen to go.

"Give us ten minutes to change, Draco. Avy and I'll come with," Noni said, standing up.

"No more than ten minutes, Noni, or I'm leaving your arse at home," Rogue informed her.

"I said ten minutes, Rogue."

"Yeah, and I grew up with you. Ten minutes could be an hour."

Noni threw her middle finger at him as she and Avy left to get ready.

"Sit on that and swivel, brother dear. I'll be out in ten minutes. And I'm not riding with you because you're an arse."

"Suits me," Rogue grinned.

Nothing changed. They still lived to wind each other up. I'd heard the stories, but I was now seeing them.

"You can ride with me anytime, beautiful," Navy shouted at her and got a blinding smile in return.

I snickered because nobody noticed how Bull had tensed at Navy's comment in all the teasing going on.

Five minutes later, the fires were put out, the trash collected, and we all headed back to the house.

Reaper said a few words while they waited for the girls to come out.

"Cuts stay on, and you watch each other's backs. Enjoy yourselves but be careful. Don't let the girls out of your sight."

"We got this, Reaper, don't worry. The girls aren't stupid, and we'll keep an eye out," Draco said, swinging his leg over his bike.

The others were doing the same.

The back door opened as Noni and Avy came out in black jeans, boots, and slinky evening tops showing tonnes of cleavage. They both had their Cuts on.

Hawk and Bull were watching them come down the back steps, their leather riding jackets swinging from their fingertips. They headed over to the shelf with helmets and picked theirs up.

"So, who am I riding with, as my brother is an arse?" Noni asked.

"You're with me, and Avy is with Hawk," Bull said, getting onto his bike and holding out his hand to her.

Avy's eyebrows rose, but she didn't say anything. She just headed over to Hawk and got on his bike.

Noni was still standing next to us, biting her lip as she considered Bull.

"You'll be safe with me," he said, still patiently waiting for her to take his hand.

I was always surprised when the uncertain part of Noni showed. Most people got the brash, over-the-top life of the party Noni. Very few ever saw the lost girl who hadn't got over the mother leaving them and her ex-husband getting locked up for life.

She must have seen something in his eyes as he sat patiently waiting for her, "Okay big guy," she said, taking his proffered hand and settling behind him on his bike.

They pulled out, and we were left watching their taillights. The gate closed behind them.

There were two prospects left behind to keep an eye on security. Reaper headed over to check on them before returning to me, where I stood waiting for him at the back door.

Grabbing me around the waist, he tossed me over his shoulder and took the stairs two at a time in a hurry to get us to our room and some privacy. By the time we hit our door, my stomach was hurting from laughing, and he was puffing slightly.

The next thing, I was bouncing on the bed after he had thrown me down on it, and Kane was pulling at my shoes and jeans, nearly pulling me off the bed in his hurry to get them off.

"Stop laughing, woman, and help me. I've been hard since you sashayed your luscious arse into the gym this morning," he growled.

Sitting up, I pulled my sweatshirt off, threw it across the room, and then attacked his belt buckle, just as desperate for him as he was for me.

Freeing his cock from the confines of his jeans, precum beaded the head of his cock. I licked his length, making him growl, before encasing him in my mouth and sucking him deep. I breathed in through my nose, relaxing my throat, taking more of him.

He groaned deep in his chest, with his hands fisted in my hair, and his breaths came hard and fast as he tried not to come.

I moaned as more precum burst over my tongue, my eyes closed, gripping his hips tightly as he slowly moved in and out of my mouth.

"Jesus, fucking… Christ. Baby, your mouth," he hissed, his hands tightening on my hair as he went to pull me off him.

I hummed, gripping him tighter and taking him deeper into my mouth. He couldn't stop himself and started thrusting faster and faster, and I took it. So turned on my thighs were wet with arousal. It would just take a little flick for me to come. Just as I was about to touch my clit Kane gave a guttural growl, "Babe, I'm about to blow," he warned me.

I nodded and pulled him towards me, wanting him to come, I needed him to come, and he did with a hoarse cry right down my throat, making me gasp for breath as I swallowed down as much as I could but still felt some dribble down my chin.

I pulled off him and grabbed my shirt to wipe my face. I knew I must be a mess. I could feel his cum and my tears running down my face.

Kane grabbed the shirt from me and gently wiped me clean, his eyes soft, warm, and relaxed.

He kissed me long and deep before his lips travelled down my neck to my breasts, where he sucked and pulled on my nipples. Tingles ran down my belly. He followed the path of the tingles until he got to the part of me that was aching with emptiness. His tongue flicked over my clit, and I clenched as his finger entered me with a thrust. My hips lifted off the bed as I writhed. I could feel my orgasm building, and I exploded just as he added a second finger.

I came back down to find myself sprawled over his chest. Pressing a kiss to it, I snuggled down, my lids slowly closing as exhaustion took me.

Perfect ending to a perfect day.

CHAPTER 21

REAPER

I woke up just as the sun rose on the horizon. My arms were full of my woman, her arm thrown over my chest and her leg nudging my already hard cock. She had blown my mind last night. I knew I should let her sleep. It had been a full-on few weeks, getting the clubhouse operational, adding security to all the business, and getting Bren, Ellie, and Ben's fostering situation sorted. Their parents still hadn't contacted anyone about them being missing, and when a visit was done, they hadn't seemed to care. I couldn't fathom that they didn't care. I was waiting for them to realise their money for the kids wouldn't be coming in. I knew we would have to be on alert.

Abby and I sat down with them and told them everything. They knew to be aware that their parents may contact them once they realised that the money wouldn't be coming in. The older two understood, but we were worried about Ellie at the primary school by herself. The school was aware of the situation and would keep an eye out.

With all the shit swirling with the ACES, I wanted to lose myself in my woman and the peace to last a little longer.

As soon as she woke up, I knew she always stilled, unsure of where she was, and then breathed deeply. She pressed a kiss to my chest before tilting her head up to me, her face soft and her eyes hazy with sleep.

Pressing my lips to hers, I deepened our morning kiss. Rolling, she took me with her. I settled between her open thighs, feeling her wet heat pressed against my aching hardness. Tilting my hips, my cock notched at the entrance to her pussy. She tightened her legs around my waist, and I slipped in further, stopping when she hissed.

"Don't stop, honey," she pleaded.

We made love slowly, I thrust gently into her. Soft kisses and gentle touches as we came.

I was pushed up on my elbows to keep my weight off her. Framing her face with my hands, I pushed her hair from her face and pressed a soft kiss to her forehead, each of her eyes and her mouth showing my love for her. Ending our kiss, I looked into her sleepy eyes. This woman had come from nowhere and wound her way quickly into my heart.

"I love you, baby," I whispered against her lips.

She tightened her arms and legs around me, pulling me tighter to her in a full-body hug. I buried my head in the crook of her neck, breathing in her scent, knowing I would take this moment with me to the end of my days.

"Love you too," she replied softly.

I would have stayed like that till the end of time, but the day had to start sometime, and ours started with Rogue knocking on the door.

"Reaper, get off the nest, brother. Need to call a meeting to discuss some shit," he bellowed through the door. He was making as if to open it by turning the handle.

"You open that fucking door, Rogue, and you're a dead man," I bellowed back at him. Nobody saw my woman like this but me.

He cackled but didn't open the door, knowing I was serious. We heard him laughing all the way down the passage.

I felt Abby's body shaking under me as she laughed.

"You lot are mad," she gasped, laughing.

I muttered at her laughter as she pushed my softening cock out of her body. I wasn't ready to leave that warm haven yet.

Pushing myself up, I dropped a kiss on her belly before getting off the bed and heading to the bathroom. Then, wetting a cloth, I returned to take care of my woman.

Tucking the blankets tight around her, I dropped a kiss on her forehead, "Go back to sleep, baby. It's not even seven yet."

"Okay, let me know what's going on later,"

I nodded and left her warm and snug in our bed where I would like to be but duty calls. I jumped in the shower, wondering what they had gotten into last night that called for a meeting at this time of the morning.

I found them all in the kitchen drinking coffee, still in their clothes from the night before. The surprise was the white-haired woman sitting stitching up Bull with what looked like a knife slash across his ribs.

"Rea?" I said with surprise.

She glanced up at me flashing me her bright green eyes, "Kane," she nodded before turning back to her stitching.

My eyes flicked to Onyx, whose eyes hadn't moved from her since I had walked into the kitchen.

I turned with concern to Draco, who was watching what we all were. I could see the questions in the eyes of the newbies who did not understand the history in the room.

"Want to tell me what happened?" I demanded.

Draco sighed, "It wasn't the ACES. Some of Rhett's crew were at the club last night. A few saw Noni arrive on the back of Bull's bike. Johnny, Adam, and Liam were there. Noni and I went and spoke to them. They were happy to see her, you know they love her, and we've never had issues with them. We left them to it and joined our crew. We figured all was cool, and it was with Rhett's older brothers. They left not long after, and baby brother got ballsy. It seems nobody told him that Rhett and Noni's divorce was Rhett's idea, not hers, and Andy started mouthing off about her being a slut and whoring around while his brother rotted in prison."

"You can imagine what that did to Noni. She's loved that little shithead from when she met him. I thought she was going to pass out. He wouldn't listen to what she was saying, and we'd had enough by then. Tried to handle it quietly, but the kid wasn't having it. A few of the older crew were pulling him back, but he had three hotheads with him. One of them had a knife, and he went for Noni but got Bull when he stepped in front of her. We sorted it out and handed them off to some of the older crew who knew the history. A couple tried to speak to Noni, but she'd checked out. And by checked out, I mean literally like when Rhett first got taken down. Got a call from Liam an hour ago to say he'd be over at eight to discuss the situation and to check on Noni."

I sighed and pulled on my neck to ease the tension already building there.

"What a cluster fuck. Where's Noni now? And why didn't one of you sew Bull up?"

Rea spoke up then, "I was at the club with some colleagues, plus I'll do a better job of this than you lot. I gave Noni a sedative and put her to bed. Avy's with her."

"You're done," she said to Bull, standing up, pulling her gloves off, and throwing them in the bin under the sink before washing her hands. Not once did she look at Onyx.

She handed me a card with a number on it. "Call me if it gets infected or bring him to A&E and ask for me. I'll get him sorted."

"Thanks, Rea," I answered, tucking the card in my wallet.

Turning to Dragon, she said, "Can you take me home, Drake?"

Dragon's eyes swivel to Onyx before he nodded, "Course, babe, no problem."

"I'll take you," Onyx stated, standing up from where he had been leaning against the kitchen wall.

Rea straightened her shoulders and looked straight at Onyx, "No, thank you. Drake, one of the others or a prospect can take me home, but not you."

Onyx closed his eyes and physically recoiled as if she'd slapped him.

We all silently watched the train smash happening in the kitchen, and we felt for them both, but Onyx had brought this on himself years ago when he was young and stupid.

"Sugar," he pleaded softly.

We watched as Rea took a stuttering breath in and paled, "Don't call me that, Milo. You lost the right to call me that six years ago. Now, I understand that last night was emotional, but you don't get to interfere in my life anymore. It's a small village, so I'm sure we'll see each other occasionally. I'll be cordial but nothing more. You broke me with what you did, and I took a long time to pull myself out of that hole. Now, I have a daughter to get home to, so if one of you could drop me home, I would appreciate it."

Dropping the bombshell of her daughter into a silent kitchen, we watched as she left out the back door. Dragon followed her but not before stopping and dropping a hand on Onyx's shoulder where he still stood near the back door, his eyes like dark pools in his pale face.

"I fucked up," he whispered as if to himself.

I sighed before going to him, dropping a heavy hand on his shoulder and shaking him slightly.

"You did, brother, and we told you so at the time. Go hit something or someone but pull yourself together. We have shit to do. Then we'll work on a plan to get you back to Rea. Yeah?"

He nodded and left the kitchen.

"All this shit before I've even had a cup of coffee," I muttered, pouring myself a cup.

"You guys have a shit tonne of drama for such a small village," Navy grinned at me.

"Tell me about it, brother, tell me about it. I'm heading to the clubhouse. Have the prospects send Liam there. I'm sure Aunt Maggie wants her kitchen back. Church at ten at the clubhouse," I informed them before leaving, with Draco following.

CHAPTER 22

DRAGON

The woman beside me was quiet but had tears streaming down her cheeks and so much pain in her face that it physically hurt looking at her.

She was still just as beautiful today as she was all those years ago when she arrived as a new student in our year nine class. With Onyx and Draco being Irish twins, we had all been in the same year at school from the start. From the beginning, Milo and Rea had hit it off and had been inseparable. Where one was, the other wasn't far away.

They had their whole lives planned out by the time we graduated from school. She went to medical school, and he was going to join the military. They would get married when she finished medical school. They didn't take into account how much war can change a man.

It had been a bad tour, and Onyx wasn't handling it well. So instead of talking about it, he decided that he needed to cut Rea loose and let her live her life free and clear of all the shit he had stored in his head.

We had tried to caution him and told him it was a bad idea. He was a stubborn fuck and set about breaking them up in the only way, and with the only person he knew she would never forgive him for. He'd done it when the rest of us weren't around to stop him or talk him down.

"He didn't do it, you know," I said softly.

She turned to look at me, wiping her face on the sleeves of her cardigan.

"Do what?"

"Sleep with Rebecca."

"Yes, he did. They sent me pictures."

"He didn't. He couldn't do it. He paid Rebecca a grand to have her say he did and rub it in your face, but he didn't sleep with her."

She sucked in a deep breath at my news.

"Why?" she wailed, her voice breaking with sobs.

"You need to ask him. We told him he was an idiot and to speak to you, but he's stubborn. He thought he was doing the right thing. He timed it well. None of us were around to stop him."

"He broke me, Drake," she whispered.

I grabbed her hand and held it tight, "Ah baby, he didn't break you. You're stronger than that."

"No, Drake, he broke me. I was going to tell him I was pregnant when she confronted me. I went into early labour. Our baby didn't stand a chance. I was only twenty weeks. So not only did I lose my baby, I lost him and all of you. I was broken. I felt I had nothing to live for. I tried for a couple of months, but nothing seemed to work, not therapy, not keeping myself busy. I couldn't pull myself out of the hole and gave up. It was just too hard to carry on. My roommates found me lying in a pool of blood. They got me help and kept it quiet. I had to take a year off school while I recovered. What really pulled me out of my funk was my mum getting ill. I had to learn to function to help my dad. Spending that year with them helped us all."

My gut tightened as I listened to her, and my heart broke for both of them. Pulling over, I stopped so I could give her my full attention.

She pulled up her sleeves and removed the thick leather cuffs on her wrists, holding her wrists up to me to show me the scars.

"It's taken years and lots of therapy to get me to where I am today."

I cupped her cheek and wiped the tears away.

"Fuck, sweetheart, I'm sorry you had to go through that alone. If we'd known what he would do, we would have stopped it. You two are like peas in a pod."

"What do you mean?" she asked.

Sighing, I wondered if I should say anything or just let sleeping dogs lie.

"Tell me, Drake, what do you mean two peas in a pod?"

I rubbed my hand over my mouth before turning to her and giving it to her straight.

"When we heard from Avy that you were getting married, Onyx lost it. He hadn't been with anyone else until then, but once he heard that, he went wild, fucking anything that looked his way, drinking hard and not being careful when we were out there.

"It was like he had a death wish. He took so many chances with his life. I still don't know how he wasn't killed. Nothing we said seemed to make a difference. It was like he gave up. Then we heard that your marriage had fallen apart and you were getting a divorce. It was like a switch flipped and stopped it all.

"He's never forgotten you, sweetheart, and I don't think he ever will. You dropping the bomb about your daughter is going to hurt him. Are you seeing someone?"

Her eyes widen at my revelations, she shook her head, "No, I'm not with anyone. I wanted a baby, and my clock was ticking. My parents left me a nice nest egg, so I had IVF. Mila is six months old and the light of my life."

"You named her Mila," I said softly.

She swallowed thickly before nodding, "Yeah. Do you want to see her?"

I smiled at her, "I do, sweetheart."

"Okay, well, take me home, and you can. I want you to know I don't go out. This was the first time I've been out for three years, and I was only there because of work."

"No judgement here, sweetheart. Who is looking after her tonight?"

"My neighbour I told her there was an emergency, so she slept the night. She looks after Mila when I have to work evenings."

I pulled into the drive of two semi-detached cottages with an abundance of plants and flowers growing in the front.

"Mary, my neighbour, loves gardening," Rea explained when I mentioned them.

I helped her out of the Land Rover and walked her to the door.

We entered quietly, and she took my hand to pull me down the small passage and into a bedroom just big enough for a cot, dresser, and changing table. All done in pink with a unicorn and rainbow mobile hanging over the cot.

I could hear soft cooing as I watched my brother's woman lean over the cot Her face no longer showing any signs of the past hurts, just love, as she reached in to pick up her daughter.

The first thing I thought as I looked at the little girl was she was beautiful, and the next was that this could be Onyx's child.

Rea's eyelashes covered her eyes as she looked down and then back up at me.

"I know," she whispered, taking Mila to the changing table. "She could be his. I didn't expect it. When she was born, for some reason, I thought she would look like me. When they handed her to me, the first thing I noticed was her black hair, and then she looked up at me with these dark eyes, and my first thought was you look just like Milo. Subconsciously I chose someone who looked like him when I made my choice. I don't regret it. She's my world."

Finishing up, she picked her up and plopped her on her hip, grabbing her little hand and waving it at me, smiling, "Say hi to Uncle Drake, Mila. He's one of the best men I know."

I snapped a quick picture before putting my phone back in my pocket.

"Do you want to hold her while I get a bottle for her?" Rea asked.

I held out my arms and took the little girl into my arms, hugging her and smelling her sweet baby scent. My heart was aching for my brother and all that he had missed. I knew this wasn't his biological daughter, but it felt like it was. I wasn't sure if he would be able to salvage this, but I would be this little girl's best uncle. I knew Rea had no family now that her parents were gone.

I met Mary, who had come in just as Mila was fussing for her bottle. She headed home not long after, and I spent the rest of the morning with them until I got a text about Church.

We'd discussed the drugs in the area and what she had noticed at the hospital.

Before leaving, I made sure that Rea had all our numbers, including Onyx's, even if she never used them.

Standing, I hugged Rea tight and dropped a kiss on Mila's head.

"Call if you ever need anything, Rea. Is it okay if I come and visit again?"

She smiled at me, "You can visit whenever you want, Drake. Just drop me a text to make sure we're home."

Nodding with agreement, I got in the Land Rover, waving at the two of them standing in the doorway. Rea's white hair mingled with the black of Mila's. I took a quick picture for my brother before reversing out of the drive and headed home.

I'd help him fix this but not until after I laid some major hurt on him for what he did.

CHAPTER 23

REAPER

Opening up the clubhouse, I saw that the prospects had been in to clean up and stock up the bar. The seating area, pool tables, and darts area had all been set up. Pushing open the door to the meeting room, I was again taken aback at the dedication Sam had put into the table. It was fucking awesome. Closing and locking that door, I went into my office. This was going to be better than trying to run shit from the dining room at the house.

A couple of prospects, Skinny and Cairo, came in carrying boxes of shit for the kitchen.

I tipped my chin to acknowledge them.

"Pres."

"Put some coffee on. I have a guy named Liam coming in. Irish, blond, and covered in tattoos. Bring him to the office when he arrives if the VP isn't with him."

"Will do, Pres," Skinny assured me as he unpacked the boxes they'd brought.

I left them to it.

Heading back to the office, I sat back and contemplated the large map of the area on the far wall with pins stuck in it at the different sites we had been to. We will be hitting them this Thursday. I just had to figure out how to do it and keep us out of the shit while doing it. I had an idea starting to form, but I would know more after I had spoken to Liam.

Not long after, there was a knock on the door, and I looked up as it opened to see Skinny in the doorway with Liam behind him.

"Pres, your visitor."

"Thanks, Skinny. Bring us some coffee before you head out."

"Will do, Pres."

I got up as Liam entered the room and held my hand out to him. I grinned when I saw him looking around at the old barn and our changes.

"Liam, it's good to see you."

"You too, Reaper. Fuck, you haven't changed at all. And this place is looking great. I hear you had a young lad do the woodwork. It looks fantastic," he said as he sat down.

"Thanks. We're happy with it. And it's not just any lad. He's my lad."

Liam's eyes widened as he looked at me in surprise.

"No shit. I didn't realise. Noni never said you had a kid."

"I don't, he's my woman's son, but as we're getting married, he's now mine."

He nodded his head in understanding.

"I get you. I wanted to come and apologise for last night. Andy has been sent to the family in Ireland to get his shit sorted out."

I shrugged before answering, "It's all good with us. Nobody was seriously hurt. Bull is tough, and Rea stitched him up, so there are no problems on our end. Appreciate the apology, though."

We sat and talked shit for a while, catching up on what had been happening in our town, what he had seen, and where his family was in the next town. We'd never had an issue with the Irish, even if we didn't always agree with their income methods. They were good people. I was curious as to what Liam wanted, though.

"So Liam, what is it I can do for you? The catch-up has been good, but I'm guessing this isn't a social call?"

He laughed and shook his head.

"Not much gets by you, does it?"

"Not if I can help it. It keeps me breathing longer if I know what I'm up against."

He rubbed his hand across his chin, looking up at the ceiling before sitting up straight in his chair and looking me straight in the eye.

"Not sure if you're aware that we have gone legit?"

I nodded. Noni had let us know.

"Noni mentioned it. Still not sure what I can do for you, though?"

He sighed, looking down at his feet.

"It's been harder than expected to keep everyone employed. The guns brought in lots of cash but going legit is taking time. I knew we needed to make changes when Rhett was put away for twenty years. There's been lots of opposition, not the least from my Da.

"The security side is doing well and growing. We've got a chance to buy into a couple of nightclubs in our town that we do security for. Unfortunately, we're strapped for cash, and I don't want to take a loan from the bank."

"You're looking for us to bankroll you?"

He nodded, "Either as a loan that we pay you back or as silent partners, the MC gets a percentage of the profits we make.

Tipping my chair back, I thought about this. I'd need to bring it to the table before making decisions.

Turning my attention back to Liam, I studied him. Being in charge of his crew showed the weariness I saw on his face.

"Bring me a business proposal and how much the buy-in is. Then, I need to take it to the table and speak to Bella about finances. Once I have all the information, we'll make a decision. It shouldn't take too long before you have your answer."

He grinned at me, "Thanks, man. I'll get the information to you this week for Bella to go over."

"Good. Now before you head out, I want to ask a favour. I'm guessing you know about us working to take out the ACES?"

He nodded at me.

"How many of your men do you think would be willing to wear our patches this Thursday at the Corvus Pub?"

Liam cocked his head to the side as he studied me, "How many do you need?"

"We need fourteen, one to cover each of us. They need to look similar to us from behind and be able to ride our bikes. We'll put you in the VIP section behind the bar, so people will see you but not who you are. Then as we each come in through the back, once we've done what we have to do, we exchange cuts, and your guys slip into the crowd. Hopefully, no one is the wiser."

He hummed as he thought it over before nodding.

"Yeah, I reckon we can make it work."

"Good," I replied. "I will also need to hire your company as bouncers on a permanent contract. I can't leave Avy unprotected, and there aren't enough of us to go around and take out the ACES."

He grinned at me, "Man, I didn't expect this when I came to apologise, and yes, of course, no problem. I'll have Adam contact Avy and sort out the contracts. When do you need us to start?"

"Is tomorrow night too soon?" I asked.

"No, it should be fine. I'll let Adam know. What's happening Thursday?" Liam asked.

"Best you don't know," I replied. "Although for you guys at the pub, it will be okay. Avy has booked a kick-ass band and is having drinks at half price as we've been shut so long. She is advertising it as opening night. It should be busy."

"Okay, no worries. Let me know if you need me to do anything and where you want to meet us to pick up your cuts and bikes," Liam said, standing up and offering me his hand.

"It's been good to see you, Reaper. Glad you boys all made it back safe and sound."

"Me too, man, me too."

We're just heading out into the main room when Cairo comes running up.

"Pres, you best come. I think Dragon is going to kill Onyx."

"For fuck's sake," I muttered as we hurriedly headed back towards the house. We hear them before we see them.

I got to say it's not often Dragon lost his temper, but when he did, it was something to see, and he was laying into Onyx, who seemed to have given up and was taking whatever was being handed to him.

The rest of the men were standing around watching. I noticed money was being passed around as bets were made. I shook my head, stopping next to Draco, tilting my head in query at the men fighting on the ground in front of us.

Onyx was getting his arse handed to him.

Draco shrugged before replying to my silent query.

"Dragon came back from dropping Rea home, grabbed Onyx by the back of his shirt, pulled him outside, and this is the result. Onyx initially fought back, but Dragon has been shouting at him the whole time, and we finally realise it's about what he did to Rea. Not sure what set Dragon off, but I'm guessing it's something he found out."

Sighing, I waded in and grabbed Dragon, pulling him off Onyx.

"Dragon, you need to calm your arse down. He's not even fighting back. You're going to kill him at this rate."

Dragon shook me off before advancing on Onyx again but stopped just before he got to him, pointed his finger in his face, and snarled at him.

"You didn't deserve her then, and you sure as shit don't deserve her now. I'm giving you this one warning, brother. She's been through enough. If you don't mean to do right by her this time, then you need to stay away."

Onyx swatted at Dragon's finger before sneering at him. "Why? Do you want her? You've always had a thing for her, haven't you?"

Dragon shook his head and looked sadly at him, "I don't want her, never like that. She's a sister like Avy, Noni, and Bella.

"Ask me what her daughter's name is, Onyx. Go on, ask me?" Dragon shouted.

"Fine, what's her daughter's name Dragon," Onyx yelled back at him.

"Mila."

It's like the air was sucked out from all of us that grew up in this village. Even Liam looked surprised.

"What's up with the name?" Navy asked.

"It's the female version of Onyx's legal name," Draco replied.

Dragon grabbed his phone from where it was lying on his Cut on the bench behind us. We all felt our phones vibrate as the pictures he took while he was with Rea came through.

I looked up to see tears running down Onyx's face as he looked at what we were seeing.

Dragon went to him and pulled him in close.

"You fucked up, brother, but we're going to fix this, I promise."

"Jesus, you guys really do have a shed load of drama in this small town of yours," Hawk muttered. "Think I've seen more action and fighting in the last three weeks here with you than in my last three months in Afghanistan."

We burst out laughing, and the whole mood changed. I walked Liam to his vehicle, and we arranged to get together Monday. The rest of us headed to church to sort out Thursday's last-minute changes.

CHAPTER 24

REAPER

We've had a busy week organising shit for what was about to go down. Liam had come through with fourteen guys he trusted that would wear our cuts and ride our bikes from the Manor to the pub, making it look like we had been at the pub the whole time. They would be collected at the end of the night or catch a taxi, whichever was easiest.

While I wasn't keen on them being in the pub unprotected, other than Dog, Abby, Noni, Avy, and Maggie had said it would seem strange that none of the women was there for anyone catching a glimpse into the VIP room.

For the most part, Avy would be behind the bar, and Liam had come through with three bouncers. So far, they seemed to be working out.

Currently, we were all lying in wait, watching the labs we had set to blow with explosives last night. We were watching to ensure there wouldn't be civilians there. We only wanted to hit the ACES, not anyone else.

Checking my watch, I saw it was 21:00 hrs and was now fully dark.

Grabbing my phone out of my pocket, I sent a message to the rest that I would blow mine at 21:10, and then they were to blow theirs at ten-minute intervals giving us time to move out to the next site. We had gone out in pairs. I had Cairo with me. We would hit as many sites as we could tonight. We were hoping for total chaos once the first lab went up.

My watch flashed 21:10, and I nodded to Cairo to press the button. We watched as the entire warehouse blew up. Quickly we crawled out of the ditch we had hidden in and raced to our vehicle. Jumping in, we took off for the next site.

Like clockwork, we saw another yellow ball light up the sky ten minutes later.

"Yesss, take that, you fuckers," Cairo whooped next to me. Making me laugh. It felt good to be doing something other than watching for a change.

We made it to the next site, and that's how our night went. Once we had blown all twenty sites we'd been watching, we drove back to the pub, taking turns cleaning our faces of camouflage and changing into clean clothes.

Parking at the back near the bikes, we each slipped silently into the VIP section of the pub, and Liam's crew, other than Liam, slipped out into the main part of the pub to join the rest of the punters with no one the wiser.

Looking around for Abby, I noticed she wasn't in the VIP room.

Grabbing Noni's arm, "Where's Abby?" I asked.

She patted my hand, smiling, "Relax, Reaper, she's behind the bar with Avy. They needed extra help, and Abby volunteered."

I nodded in relief before heading out to check on her. I watched as she helped Avy serve until there was a lull in customers. Sneaking up behind her, I wrapped my arms tight around her and pressed a kiss to her neck, making her shiver.

"You'd best be careful. My man is the jealous type," she said, tilting her head against my shoulder and grinned up at me.

"Is that right? I don't blame him, babe. If you were mine, I'd be hanging onto you tight." I pressed another kiss to her lips, wishing we were anywhere but there.

"Everything okay?" Avy questioned, coming over.

"Yeah," I replied. "How much longer until the last call?"

"Only another ten minutes, the band is winding down. It's been a good night, not many hassles. Liam's guys are good at what they do."

"That's great news, one less thing for us to worry about. I'm still going to be sending one of the prospects with you for the evening shift. I don't want you leaving here by yourself," I told her. My sister's sensible, so I wasn't surprised when she nodded agreeably.

"Whatever you want, Reaper, I'm not going to complain about having extra hands to help. Let me just get the bell for the last call, and we can start clearing up. There have been lots of blues and twos going past the last couple of hours. I want to get home and check the news."

She gave me a little smirk before grabbing the handle on the old bell we had hanging behind the bar and ringing the shit out of it, shouting *last call.*

Abby and I laughed at the stampede that hit the bar. I let my woman go so that she could help Avy. I noticed that the entire MC was out and mingling, ensuring that our faces were seen. Dog and Maggie were taking a turn around the dance floor to the last song of the evening.

Bull grabbed Noni and pulled her onto the floor with him. She was smiling as he twirled her around. Hard to believe a man that size could move so smoothly.

The prospects were going around collecting glasses without having to be told. So far, they had been a good fit. I knew Skinny would be as he was Bull's younger brother.

Draco, Rogue, Dragon, Onyx, and I chatted with the locals that knew us. Then, if the police came calling, we would have a solid alibi. Not that we expected any pushback from this, we'd been careful.

Navy and Cairo jumped behind the bar and pushed Avy towards Hawk and Abby my way. We joined the others on the dance floor as the band played another song.

It had been a good night, although I couldn't wait to get my woman back to the manor.

An hour later and the pub was closed for the night. A couple of Liam's guys drove our vehicles back to the manor, where their guys would pick them up.

The rest of us started our bikes, and as I pulled out of the Corvus Pub parking lot, my woman wrapped tight around me, my brothers falling in around us. I couldn't help but think that *'Life was good.'*

The End

Acknowledgements

I would like to say a massive thank you to my Beta Readers Cloe Rowe and Clare. F. you ladies rock.

To my husband for always encouraging me on whatever crazy idea takes me at the time. Being there for me, always putting me first and for treating me like a queen. After 27 years you are still my inspiration.

My eldest daughter Helen offered positive quotes and comments daily during this journey. I love you more than the whole world and don't know what I would do without you and your encouragement. Love you, baby.

To my youngest, my lovely Ria, I love your snarky comments when we have to share the same space while I write. Don't ever change. Love you to the moon and back.

To my mum who keeps our house running smoothly, I honestly don't know what I would do without you. Love you.

To all my readers who took a chance on me with my first book Wild & Free and for reaching out with positive comments and suggestions.

One last thing .... **REVIEWS** feed an author's soul, and we learn and grow from them. Whether it be just a rating left or a few words they are what pushes us to keep writing.

About the Author

I grew up on a cattle farm on the outskirts of a small town in Zambia, Southern Central Africa. I went to school in South Africa, Zambia and finally finished my schooling in Zimbabwe. I had an amazing childhood filled with fantastic experiences. As a family, we often went on holiday to Lake Kariba and I feel very privileged to have seen Victoria Falls, one of the seven wonders of the world several times.

My grandparents lived on the same farm as my parents and me. It was my grandmother, my Ouma who first introduced me to the romance genre by passing her Mills and Boons on to me, and I was hooked from there.

I now live happily in Jane Austen country in the UK with my family, VA by day and wordsmith by night.

Follow me:

Email: michelledups@yahoo.com

https://www.facebook.com/michelle.dups.5/

https://www.instagram.com/author_michelle_dups

www.michelledups.carrd.co

https://www.goodreads.com/michelledups

NEXT BOOK IN SERIES

Sanctuary Series

Sanctuary Book 2 - ANGEL (Kyle and Lottie's story)

Sanctuary Book 3 – Julie (Julie & Joel)

Sanctuary Book 4 – Amy a Novella.

Sanctuary Book 5 – The Russos – Autumn 2023

Crow MC

Reaper Book 1

Onyx Book 2

Rogue Book 3

Draco Book 4 – August 2023

Dragon Book 5 – December 2023

Avy Book 6 – February 2024

Noni Book 7 - TBC

Navy Book 8 - TBC

Printed in Great Britain
by Amazon